Maple and Spice

Maple

and

Spice

Moushmi Biswas

Cover shows Amrita Sen: musician, designer and entrepreneur
amritasen.com

Matador
9 Priory Business Park,
Wistow Road, Kibworth Beauchamp,
Leicestershire. LE8 0RX
Tel: 0116 279 2299
Email: books@troubador.co.uk
Web: www.troubador.co.uk/matador
Twitter: @matadorbooks

ISBN 978 1789013 399

British Library Cataloguing in Publication Data.
A catalogue record for this book is available from the British Library.

Printed and Bound in the UK by 4Edge Limited
Typeset in 11pt Minion Pro by Troubador Publishing Ltd, Leicester, UK

Matador is an imprint of Troubador Publishing Ltd

To Dillon

1

Monisha Bastikar was the most marriageable Indian woman in Vermont: twenty-seven years old, newly qualified as a doctor, and with no boyfriends current or previous. Prospects were usually good for female medics. They had recession-proof careers and guaranteed incomes, but there was a downside. After years of study, she had slipped into an age bracket considered less appealing, the late twenties. As she stared into her bedroom mirror, familiar fears crept in. Her celebration party was tomorrow and where were all the men?

Each time an eligible bachelor from the community got hitched, her heart fluttered with wild panic. Last summer it was Rahul Acharya, the handsome accountant, who had eloped with his Vietnamese cleaning lady. Shock, horror! A few months later, Dr Ravi Sinha proposed to his new intern. Thump! Thump! Then, millionaire Vinal Verma finally abandoned his footlose and fancy free lifestyle and found himself a gorgeous Gujarati wife. Only Sohan Singh was left now. The dentist with a lifetime driving ban.

"My daughter shall not be his taxi," her mother had said. And with that the family's proposal was instantly rejected.

But it was no use being picky now. Her residency in Boston was just around the corner, and when it started, each year would melt away like snow on Mount Mansfield. What if she woke up one day and found herself lying in a heap alongside the untouchables of the marriage market? The dreaded thirty-pluses. Dear God, she would have to find someone soon.

Monisha jumped as her mother entered the room. When Monisha saw the boxes of saris and sparkling jewellery arrive, she turned her face away.

"What's the point of making an effort when there are no available men?"

"Presentation! Presentation!" cried Mrs Leela Bastikar, as she chose for herself a peacock-blue sari. "Mustn't ignore it. Somebody there might know of someone suitable. Word of mouth is always best."

Monisha held up the floor-length skirt and cropped blouse of a cream-and-silver chanya-choli, and caught a nod of approval. But, as her mother's eyes travelled upwards, across her face and to the top of her head, panic set in again. At five foot seven she stood neck and neck with most Indian men. Why did she have to be so darn tall?

"WITH FLAT SANDALS," shouted Mrs Bastikar before rushing off to practise her American pronunciations.

"Now you look purr-fect!"

As Monisha placed the outfit in her wardrobe, tears trickled down her face. Soon she would be abandoning the soothing magnolia walls of her bedroom for sterile space in an apartment at North End, five minutes from St Anthony's hospital. At a whopping $1,150 a month.

The comfortable sameness of the last twenty years would instantly vanish. The classical Indian dance lessons with big-bottomed Mrs Bhatia. Twirling on hardwood floors to sitar tapes. Ankle bells jingling. There would be none of that in Boston. No weekly dinner parties either. Samosas and cutlets to start. Parents raving about their sons and daughters. Pilau rice and chicken for the main course. *Saturday Night Live* to finish.

She could almost smell the fumes of peaty malt whisky and cigarettes, see the women fretting over turmeric stains and hear the drunken laughter of men, drowning in Johnnie Walker and nostalgia.

"America has skyscrapers and sidewalks, but India has a soul."

"Why are you here, then?" her father would ask. His best friend, Saurav Das, always came up with an answer.

"Doesn't the physics professor know that we're all just greyhounds chasing a hunk of meat?"

From childhood to adulthood, Monisha had always attended the gatherings religiously, though they were repetitive. Stifling even. But why get caught up in the chaos and spend Saturday nights in town, wobbling round in high heels, when there was a higher purpose? Her three shining goals: to become a wife, a board-certified physician and a mother of two.

Monisha looked in the mirror again. Thump! Thump! She had to find a husband. Without a husband, two out of three of her life goals were unachievable, and unless she devised a whole new set of aspirations, she'd go down as a failure. Gulp!

On the night of her party, the Belvedere Hotel was in full swing. Lake Champlain, its stunning backdrop, dazzled in the fiery glow of the setting sun. The foyer was crammed with taffeta-clad blondes, sipping cocktails. The Bastikars proceeded to the ballroom, where a 'CONGRATULATIONS' sign swung from the ceiling, propped up by multicoloured balloons. Each table was draped in gold cloth, and studded with tea lights and scented candles. At the back of every chair hung a droopy red organza bow.

Monisha surveyed the scene before her. It seemed an awful lot of fuss for nothing. But she could never have stopped her mother and father from celebrating, for it was every Indian parent's dream that at least one of their children would enter the medical profession, the noblest of them all, and amongst the Bastikars she was the first doctor.

Her brother Swanker walked past her, carrying an incense stick and a bunch of carnations. He knelt before the statue of Saraswati, the goddess of learning and placed both at her feet.

"That's my boy!" cooed Mrs Bastikar, rushing over and pinching his cheeks.

Monisha rolled her eyes. 'Good old Swanker.' Perpetual party animal. Blundering through engineering school between retakes, but still the apple of his mother's eye. And his send-off would be even better than this one.

4

As the night sky descended, the guests assembled in the ballroom. The evening began with a short prayer, after which Mr Vinod Verma, president of the Indian Cultural Society grabbed the microphone. As usual, there was feedback.

"Good evening ladies and gentlemen-entlemen. Thank you-ank you to those who have made their generous, tax-free donations to our society-iety." The screeching noises forced him to pause. "We are gathered here today-ay to celebrate Monisha's achievement. We wish her a long and successful career-eer in medicine. Congratulations to Leela and Amit Bastikar for raising-aising such a beautiful, brilliant daughter-aughter. Best wishes to you Monisha-isha."

Monisha blushed as she collected a bouquet of red roses. Champagne glasses clinked. Kebabs and canapes were guzzled down. After dinner, the newly qualified 'Doctor Bastikar' floated across the ballroom like a cream-and-silver cloud, periodically pausing to make small talk with guests. Eventually, she caught her mother speaking to the president.

"I've asked around Leela, but I couldn't find anyone willing to come forth," said Mr Verma through wine stained lips.

"No one at all?" asked Mrs Bastikar. "Cousins, brothers, friends, nephews… no one?"

"One or two… But they wanted proper Indian girls." His eyes lowered gradually, ultimately settling on his shiny, new brogues. "And, er, slightly younger."

Monisha noticed the sudden flash of anger on her mother's face. Her ears pricked up.

"But she's a doctor now, Verma-ji, and more Indian than the girls back home."

Mr Verma shook his head. "They all become Americanised, Leela, however much you try to save them. They go to college, get boyfriends... they drink... they smoke in secret... and most of them are not even virgins!"

Leela Bastikar hissed loudly and began marching towards her daughter. "Monisha. Come here and talk to Mr Verma!"

The eavesdropping was over. Monisha took slow, hesitant steps over to the president.

"Do you drink alcohol?" asked Mrs Bastikar, punctuating her words with a piercing stare.

Monisha shook her head, "I've tried wine once or twice."

"Do you smoke?"

Vinod Verma shifted uncomfortably in front of the two ladies.

"Mom, you know I don't. What is this?"

Mrs Bastikar cut in, her voice deafeningly loud. "Have you ever had a boyfriend?"

"You know I haven't." Monisha was beginning to feel queasy.

"HAVE YOU EVER SLEPT WITH A MAN?"

The sentence echoed through the ballroom. A clique of sari-clad women lifted their heads. Immediately, she felt Vinod Verma's snake-like eyes upon her.

"NEVER!"

"You are indeed a good Indian girl, Monisha," said Mr Verma, before dashing off towards his friends.

Monisha glared at her mother, her face now beetroot red. But Mrs Bastikar simply turned her back and began walking swiftly, towards the waiters. Thankfully, Monisha found a side door, through which she managed to slip out. Going down a flight of steps, she found her way into the luxurious Belvedere bathrooms.

The spacious disabled cubicle contained a white wicker chair. Monisha hiked up her skirt and plonked herself on it, fuming. Everything was so futile! Attending dinner parties. Avoiding drunken nights out and boyfriends. Protecting her reputation. For nothing! No man was interested. What was the point of being good when nobody believed you?

It seemed like years before she was back in the safety of her bedroom. In front of her dressing table mirror, she sat. Mascara-soaked tears dripped down her face. At the sound of short, arthritic footsteps down the corridor, Monisha shot up and dried her eyes.

Mrs Bastikar knocked on the door. There was no response. She cautiously entered the room.

"How could you embarrass me like that?" Monisha scowled.

Mrs Bastikar walked across the room, picking up mascara-stained tissues off the floor as she went.

"That silly ass needed to be taught a lesson."

Monisha sighed.

"At least he was honest. There is no one."

Her mother placed both hands on her shoulders.

"Nonsense, Monisha. There are millions of men in India. You can take your pick!"

Millions of men? Now that was a comforting thought.

Maybe her dream could become a reality: a wedding at the Mumbai Taj. Real sitar music echoing through the grand ballroom. The delicate scent of rose petals and jasmine. There she would be, sitting like a queen on the bridal throne next to her tall, handsome, dignified husband.

All she had to do now was go and find him.

2

It was half past five and the café was buzzing with office workers. The counter was stacked with magazines, each one plastered with pictures of Princess Diana. Monisha tucked a copy under her arm and ordered a cappuccino. She took a seat by the window and nervously thumbed through the pages. Now and again she lifted her head, looking for Tina. How on earth would she break the news?

Twenty excruciating minutes later, Tina arrived. Armed with clipboards and legal files, she brushed past the suited men. Despite being polar opposites, they'd been best friends throughout school. Monisha, the mild-mannered swat and Tina, a brassy red-head who was always battling something. Usually it was alcohol, anorexia or yet another boyfriend. But, despite the drama, she sailed effortlessly through every exam, while Monisha toiled night and day. A cursory glance at a few cheat notes would earn her firsts in English language and literature and eventually a place in law school.

"This better be good," said Tina, squinting deeply at her friend after they'd exchanged hugs. "Seeing as you dragged me out here before finals."

Her eyes were reddened from all-night cramming. This wasn't the time to make small talk. That sinking feeling was beginning again. Monisha took a deep breath.

"I'm going to India to get married."

A shocked silence lingered for a while. Tina eventually raised her eyebrows and began a barrage of questions.

"Seriously? Wow! When? Who's the guy?"

"I leave on Friday. I haven't met him."

The creases on Tina's forehead coalesced into a giant frown. "Oh, so it's going to be one of those *arranged* marriages."

Monisha folded her arms. That was downright condescending from her best friend.

"I know you've talked about it, but I never thought you'd go through with it," said Tina.

"My mother is in Mumbai, shortlisting."

"Shortlisting?" The frown changed shape. "Like a recruitment firm? What about the single Indian guys here? Surely they're better than a bunch of strangers!"

"But there are no Indian guys here," replied Monisha. Sohan Singh didn't count. Tina's words jarred her a bit. Choosing from a bunch of strangers, that's what it amounted to. Millions of strangers really.

Monisha sat up straight and wiped the corners of her mouth. "I get to go out with a few guys my mom has picked and if we like each other, we both come to a decision."

Tina wasn't going to give up lightly.

"Based on how many dates?"

Monisha's initial confidence began to wither. She knew the plan, but hadn't yet fleshed out the details. How many dates would it take? She'd have to act swiftly, trust her instincts and reject the men she didn't like straight away. But what if the guy was nervous and not at his best on the first date? And if it took several dates to get him to unwind, would that mean less time with the others? Oh God! How was she going to do this?

Tina tapped her fingernails onto the table as she waited for an answer.

"I don't know, but I'll be there for a whole month."

"One month to decide? You can't be serious!"

The waitress came over to gather their trays. Monisha ordered a hot chocolate. Tina's questions were leaving a slightly bitter taste in her mouth.

"Well, after residency starts I won't have time, then I'll be too old and Indian men don't want you if you're over thirty."

"But what do you want, Monisha?" asked Tina, giving her a stare that could have cracked her head open. Monisha gazed dreamily out of the window.

What did she want? What did she want?

She wanted to get married in the traditional Indian way, raise a family and specialise, of course.

"Well, I want marriage and kids too… eventually," said Tina. "Whatever happened to meeting someone and falling in love?"

Monisha screwed up her nose and cut off her friend mid-flow.

11

"That's the American way and fifty percent of the time it ends up in divorce… and pays for your Porsche!"

Tina chuckled at the irony. It was stats like that which would certainly keep her in business.

The waitress arrived with more hot chocolate and placed it smack bang on Diana's dejected face.

"What type of guy are you looking for?" asked Tina, changing the subject.

"Indian, Brahmin… a medic with good prospects here," said Monisha, without batting an eyelid.

Tina stared harshly. "And they say Americans are racist!"

She bit her lip when she realised how it must have sounded. Her mother was the one for stereotypes. She was always harping on about white men leaving their wives and black men taking drugs.

Monisha jumbled through her explanations. She wanted to keep the family happy and make life easier. Tina moved in closer.

"Don't you want to know what he's like in bed? What if he has… er, problems?"

Americans only care about one thing, thought Monisha. She shrugged her shoulders. "That's not such a big deal."

"He could always read the *Kama Sutra*," joked Tina. The girls giggled when they remembered how they'd found the book on Professor Bastikar's desk, and seen the portly Maharajas contorting themselves.

The laughter stopped abruptly.

"I just can't imagine marrying someone who I don't love," said Tina.

"It works differently over there," said Monisha.

"Yes, but you're over here. And you have been for twenty-seven years!"

Tina's rising voice prompted angry stares from onlookers. A suited man rose up from behind his book, like a jack-in-the box. She softened her tone. "I know you learned Indian dances and Hindi, but you know how to ski and skate too."

Monisha let out a deep sigh. Her joyous bit of news was turning into a heated debate. Tina would now have to be given the explanation she had learned by rote at her mother's knee.

"I know it seems strange, but the Indian way is scientific. It's a law of the universe. Things that start off big get smaller with time, and things that start off small can grow. Love is the same."

Tina shot her a quizzical stare and sipped her coffee.

Monisha continued. "Couples here fall head over heels in love, they get married… It all starts off big and falls away gradually. There, you meet your husband and the love grows. Bit by bit."

There was another stunned silence. Tina fumbled for the right words.

"I get the theory, but don't you want to try before you buy? Especially for such a big decision."

It was getting late. The argument had to end somewhere. Monisha looked at her watch and rose from her chair. "Arranged marriages have been around for thousands of years," she said. "They've stood the test of time."

Tina stared glumly at her coffee, then swigged it down. Despite the explanations, she was none the wiser. Running off to marry a complete stranger made absolutely no sense.

Then again, she'd seen couples tie the knot after years of dating and get divorced. It wasn't science. Whichever way you did it, you made an educated guess and hoped for the best.

Monisha said her goodbyes with a saccharin-sweet hug. It didn't really matter what Tina thought. When law school was finished, she could end up anywhere.

Outside, the chilling wind blew ferociously and brought with it a clattering of hailstones. Monisha walked swiftly to her car, shaking off the icy pellets as she went.

Friends come and go, like the weather, she told herself.

Marriage and family were forever.

3

Whether it was two in the morning or two in the afternoon, Mumbai airport was jam-packed and chaotic. Scores of people piled in and out of aircrafts, across travellators, and up and down escalators: impeccable air stewardesses in single file, with their noses pointed in the air. Scruffy bandit-types claiming odd-looking parcels from baggage belts. Scraggly haired women, their wailing children and pock-marked husbands, all carried in the crush of the immigration queue.

Monisha pushed and jabbed her way into the cool arrivals hall. One giant lunge through the revolving doors and she was finally out into the spicy, sweat-filled air. Amidst the sound of spluttering machines, jingly Bollywood tunes and cries of "Taxi, taxi," she heard someone call her name. Frantically, she scanned the crowd.

Behind a group of begging children stood Aunt Romila, waving an outstretched hand and grinning.

Monisha scurried towards her. Out of nowhere, a coolie swooped in and grabbed the suitcases. As the ladies strolled across the busy pavement to the waiting jeep, he trailed behind them.

"To Sitara Road," she said to her driver. "Remember my niece from America? She's a doctor now."

He nodded approvingly.

Monisha scrambled in. No doubt they'd start discussing their ailments soon. Her stomach whirred as they hit the bumps in the road. Ugh! In just twenty minutes, the travelling would be over and the real journey would begin. She watched the men through the tinted glass, picking out suited ones from shabby workers. A man clutching a briefcase caught her eye. Then another, dressed in a tailored suit, reading a paper. Any one of them could be standing in front of her tomorrow. Thump! Thump!

The jeep screeched to a halt in front of the ramshackle, old house. There it stood, jutting out from the edge of Sitara Road, their holiday home: too ugly for fashionable Juhu. Overgrown creepers hid its paint-chipped windows, and on the rusted-iron side gates, in bold black letters, was a message for hungry realtors: 'THIS HOUSE IS NOT FOR SALE'.

Its sprawling courtyard and lop-sided rooms had been the childhood abode of Leela Bastikar, her sister Romila, and her brothers Rohit and Shyam. Over the years, the interior had been redecorated dramatically. Nowadays, the house was mainly used by the Bastikars on their visits to Mumbai. And it was to here that Mrs Bastikar had shifted for the past month to undertake her matchmaking duties.

As the weighty, wooden front door creaked open, the emerald and grey swirls on the marble floor sprang into view. Monisha stepped in and removed her shoes. Her eyes wandered round the room in search of her favourite piece of furniture, the ten-seater dining table, made of the darkest mahogany. When she saw it, her heart skipped a beat! There it lay, buried under piles of newspapers opened at the matrimonial columns. Her mother had probably spent hours trawling through them.

In the lounge room, a man with slickly oiled hair and a handlebar moustache sat slouched in an armchair. When he saw her, he rose and placed one palm against the other, in the traditional namaste greeting. She reciprocated, hoping that he wasn't a prospective bridegroom.

Suddenly, Leela Bastikar flew out of the kitchen, in a whirlwind of pink chiffon.

"How are you, Monisha?" she asked, and without waiting for an answer she waved the flat of her hand excitedly in front of the gentleman. "This is Mr Shastri, the astrologer. With his kind help, from hundreds, we have made a list of twenty. And, of these, eight have agreed to visit."

The aroma of ginger tea filled the air; a new male helper brought over a tray with four cups. Monisha eased herself onto the couch. *So, this was how millions of men, became hundreds*, she thought. *And hundreds became eight. Eight!* Her heart soared into a gallop rhythm. How was she going to do this in a month?

She'd only managed half a cup before she was whisked off to the beauty parlour down the road. Here her swollen feet were descaled, and her arms and legs waxed until they were red raw. Her overgrown eyebrows were threaded into neat arcs and her skin scrubbed with knobbly turmeric, until it lightened. All throughout the painful grooming process, she winced and groaned.

"You have to look your best, young lady," said her aunt. "The first boy is an ear, nose and throat specialist. And quite wealthy, I hear."

That night, Monisha dreamed of stunning mansions, twin sinks and garden parties. When the morning came, she was jittery. She sifted through a pile of outfits. Which one would impress the most? It had to be white. Pure, virginal white.

She chose a white salwar suit embroidered with fine gold detail. She lightened her face with more turmeric and carefully applied her makeup. After breakfast, she was instructed by her mother to stay put in her room. There she waited, staring at film magazines, listening for the hum of a car's engine. When she heard it, her heart stopped.

A moment later, the front door opened. Then came a cacophony of sounds. Shoes slapping against the marble floor. Voices. An older man's first. Her mother's. An older woman's. Her aunt's. Marathi. English. Broken English. Marathi. Hindi. Leather sofas squelching. Then spoons, glasses and cups clinking.

Finally, the sound of her own name echoed from the stairwell.

She took a deep breath and descended as gracefully as she could, pretending not to notice the grey-haired man and woman sitting on the sofa.

"Monisha, please welcome Dr and Mrs Shirke," said Leela Bastikar in a sugary voice, completely unlike her own.

"Namaste," said Monisha. As she bent her head and folded her palms, she noticed the gentleman's Ralph Lauren shirt.

Dr and Mrs Shirke rose in unison and returned her greeting. They studied her closely and curled their lips into tentative smiles. Instantly, she felt as if something was wrong. Then came overwhelming dread. They didn't like what they saw. *They didn't like her.*

Dr Shirke forced himself to speak. "So, are you all set for residency?"

Monisha met his gaze briefly. "I guess so." She glanced down at the marble floor and followed its elaborate swirls. *What was wrong with her?*

Dr Shirke turned directly towards her mother, and launched into a monologue about the impact of globalisation on Mumbai and the death of small business. Small businesses were apparently the back bone of India. Monisha was only half listening. After ten minutes, he looked up at the clock and glanced sideways at his wife, who nodded submissively.

"So sorry, Mrs Bastikar," he shook his head. Monisha froze.

"But we have to make our way now. We are going to a lunch party and… with the traffic."

Leela Bastikar nodded enthusiastically.

"Of course! Peak hour, rush hour, Saturday afternoon – traffic all the time."

Once more, the couple rose in unison. Mrs Bastikar escorted them to the door, where they stopped to put on their shoes. "You have our number," she said.

"Yes," replied Dr Shirke. He turned back towards Monisha. "Best of luck… with everything."

An eerie silence descended across the room.

"What was that all about?" asked Monisha, feeling a mixture of rejection and relief when they'd gone. "And where was their son?"

Aunt Romila called for another pot of tea. "Usually the boy's parents come to see the girl first and if they like her, they arrange another meeting."

"They seemed nice," said Leela Bastikar.

Her sister shook her head vehemently. "Just a rich family with high expectations. Didn't you notice they were both fair skinned and that he was short?"

"So, I was too dark and too tall for them," said Monisha. It made sense now, the disappointment in their faces.

Aunt Romila sipped her tea quietly. It was a while before she spoke.

"Don't be upset, Monisha. You have to be prepared for this... Besides, you might do the same to someone else."

"Tomorrow is another day," said Leela Bastikar, shrugging her shoulders.

All afternoon Monisha sulked in front of the television. Dinner came and went; she excused herself after a few mouthfuls. When she saw the freshly ironed salwar suit in her room, ready for the next day, she tossed it on the floor. All along she'd assumed that she would be the one making the choices. How utterly stupid of her. She had completely forgotten to consider that a man would have to like her too.

And, in India, before anything else, she would have to get past his parents.

4

Two days later came promising news. The next young bachelor from Mrs Bastikar's shortlist had been orphaned at the age of eight. That meant no parents! His sister would be accompanying him instead.

On the day of his arrival, there was pandemonium. The helper was sent back and forth to the market in search of the best Darjeeling tea. The marble floor was scrubbed and polished so often that Aunt Romila slipped. Monisha had stayed in her room all morning, trying on outfits that were too tight or too loose. But, after what seemed like hours of preparation, everything happened in a split-second. The doorbell rang, Aunt Romila called her name and she bolted out, without her slippers.

From the top of the stairs she could see a scruffy-looking man with mullet-style hair. Tall, thin and dark skinned, he wore an oversized, checked jacket and white running shoes. First, he slid down the sofa. Then, rather annoyingly, he began tapping it with his fingers.

Monisha made her way down and greeted her guests. The man's sister began the conversation with a nervous jumble of words, about the weather, the traffic and the swirly marble floor. It was a while before anyone else could get a word in.

Between mouthfuls of samosas and sips of Darjeeling tea, the woman spoke about the loss of her parents and her struggle to raise her brother alone. She'd fought tooth and nail to get him educated. Now, to her credit, he'd become a doctor and passed the US exams. Unfortunately, this meant he might leave her. She dabbed her eyes with a handkerchief.

Monisha listened sympathetically. She imagined being married to the young man. First, they'd have to visit the hairdresser, then the menswear department. On the plus side, there would be no in-laws, apart from his over-protective sister.

Suddenly, her trail of thoughts was interrupted when she felt something rustling against her palm. It was a CV.

His exam scores were abysmal. Utterly, utterly abysmal.

But Monisha didn't want to make him feel like the Shirkes had made her feel; she hid her dismay and smiled sweetly. Ask him something, she told herself. Anything!

Except to do with exams. Or residency, which he'd never make.

"What do you like doing in your spare time?"

"I like danthing".

Heavens above, he had a lisp as well! Danthing? Her list was expanding. A new hairstyle, a new wardrobe, an exam re-sit and speech therapy. This was going to be impossible!

She gulped down a samosa. Perhaps he'd just mispronounced the word. She could ask him another question to check. It would have to be work-related. She was running out of ideas.

"Have you applied for jobs?"

"I didn't get into residenthy this time round."

There was a deathly silence. Leela Bastikar broke it by offering everyone another round of tea. They all declined. "Monisha will be starting at St Anthony's when she goes back."

"In Boston," she added.

Monisha stared down at her feet and then at the swirly marble floor. How did her mother manage to choose such awkward moments?

The man's sister clambered up from the couch. "He'll be applying again," she said, fidgeting with her handbag.

Monisha shook the young man's hand. A confusing current of emotions hit her at once. Did she want to see him again? There were positives: no in-laws and he was teetotal. But his prospects were limited. His lisp too audible. She felt sorry for him, but that couldn't be a sound basis for a marriage.

"Best of luck," she blurted.

Her stomach churned when she realised she'd delivered the same parting words as Mr Shirke, with the same hint of smugness and finality.

An uncomfortable silence lingered as the sibling pair made their way to the door with heads bowed low.

"It's all so cruel," said Monisha when they'd gone. "He must feel awful."

"Don't waste your sympathy, Monisha," warned Aunt

Romila as she rushed off to pay her obligatory weekly visit to her in-laws. "Young doctors like him get snapped up in an instant."

At midday, the hallway phone began ringing. Someone was calling to cancel a meeting and they didn't wish to rebook. Mrs Bastikar looked a little nervous. Half an hour later, it happened again. Another cancellation. She held the corner of her sari and wiped the sweat off her brow. Time was passing, and the number of suitors was rapidly diminishing.

Ten minutes later, the phone rang once more. Leela Bastikar clutched her chest and traipsed towards it, heavy hearted. Within seconds her face broke out into an enormous smile. "Someone is coming this afternoon!" she screeched at the top of her lungs. "The uncle of the boy from Connecticut."

The helper raised his eyebrows and mumbled something about not having an appointment. Monisha voiced her own concerns. How would they manage without Aunt Romila?

Leela Bastikar waved them off, then struggled up the stairs. There was no time, she said, groaning as her knees cracked. No time to lose! They were four suitors down and right now she absolutely had to change her sari.

Her guest was a Mr Sunil Vanjare, the paternal uncle of the strongest contender so far, Rajesh Vanjare, a radiologist from Connecticut. The Vanjare family lived in Pune, a couple of hours away by train. Sunil Vanjare had business in Mumbai, so he promised his brother, the father of Rajesh, that he'd call in on the Bastikars.

When the doorbell rang, Monisha jumped up. She'd been under strict orders to remain upstairs in her room.

But, there, she felt excluded. She needed a hideout, from where she could at least listen in. After hunting around, she found a bulky wooden chest, which she managed to drag onto the landing, to crouch behind.

Sunil Vanjare arrived at the door at quarter past three. He wore a starched cotton dhoti and carried a hand-carved walking stick. And he seemed a delightful old man as he described every minute of his journey over, in a warm melodic voice.

He told Mrs Bastikar that the Vanjares were a highly traditional family and that he was its current head, which is why his brother had asked him to pay them a visit. He was always choosing brides for relatives and writing advertisements in matrimonial columns, but weddings were becoming a chore. Last year he'd been to twelve. Nothing annoyed him more than having to come back and forth to Mumbai to collect his rent money from the bank. Why the matter couldn't be dealt with in Pune he did not know. Banks were a complete nuisance, he complained.

When he saw Leela Bastikar glance up at the clock, Sunil Vanjare changed the topic. "Rajesh is a perfect gentleman. Ever since he was born, he has brought us nothing but joy! He could have chosen to study in Delhi or Bangalore, but he preferred to be near us, so he stayed in Pune."

Mrs Bastikar smiled and called for tea.

"There is nothing in the world like Darjeeling tea," said Sunil Vanjare, as the helper placed a tray of coconut sweets and a freshly made pot in front of him. "I can't imagine drinking it out of a bag."

"You mean a tea bag!" laughed Leela Bastikar.

Sunil Vanjare sipped his tea contentedly, then slipped a coconut sweet into his mouth.

"I have a picture of Rajesh."

He fumbled around in his pockets, unable to locate the photo. He stood up and emptied his side pockets. A lone bunch of keys fell onto the table.

From that moment on there was chaos.

The old man jigged about and shook his dhoti to and fro. Nothing. He swung it wildly from side to side. Nothing. He searched his front pocket. Nothing. He felt his side pockets again. Nothing. Finally, he let out an anguished cry.

"MY WALLET! MY WALLET! It's gone. I must have been pickpocketed."

What was he to do without his wallet? How would he get home? He could go to the State Bank and take money out. But he had no ID on him now. Perhaps, if he saw the teller who'd served him that morning, she would recognise him. It was running late. Would he make it in time? He began trembling.

Leela Bastikar listened patiently and tried to calm him down. She suggested that he call his family and pointed him in the direction of the telephone.

"No point, no point! Nobody is home now!" he yelled before collapsing into the armchair with his head in his knees. His shirt was now drenched with sweat, his scant hair stringy and wet.

From behind the chest, Monisha watched her mother pull out a stack of hundred-rupee notes from her own purse.

After much cajoling, the old man took the money. Mrs Bastikar called for a helper.

"You can always pay it back when your brother comes to visit with Rajesh."

When the helper arrived, Sunil Vanjare was heaved up off the chair and handed his walking stick. He shuffled slowly towards the door.

"Thank you for your kindness. Our family will remember this always."

Monisha took in a deep breath and rose up from her hiding place. It had been a strange day. Tea and samosas with Mr Lisper and his sister, two cancellations, an unexpected visitor, and then the dramatic scene in the lounge.

"That poor man!" she said as she hurtled down the staircase towards her mother. "He must have been pickpocketed when he returned from the bank… but then how did he pay for the cab ride over?"

Mrs Bastikar shifted uncomfortably in her chair.

"Perhaps we could discuss this later with Uncle Rohit."

The grandfather clock chimed solemnly five times. Uncle Rohit would be here any minute for a snack and a cup of tea. With his flabby arms, round face and protruding belly, he was heading towards diabetes, his doctor had warned. In spite of it, whenever he visited, Leela Bastikar would stuff her little brother with the fattening treats he was forbidden from eating in his own home.

As soon as he arrived, she placed a bowl of thick, creamy rice pudding in front of him. While he tucked in, she relayed the afternoon's events.

Uncle Rohit listened, making occasional slurping noises. When he finished the final mouthful, he asked for a glass of water and swigged it down noisily. "It's obvious you've been scammed, Leela," he said. "Count yourself lucky he didn't take your jewellery."

Monisha and her mother exchanged horrified looks. Leela Bastikar shook her head in disbelief. "No, it can't be!"

Monisha felt her knees wobble to jelly. A wave of nausea swept through her. Fear was a lump in her throat as she watched Uncle Rohit pick up the telephone and dial the contact number for Rahul Vanjare. She waited with bated breath as he spoke to the boy's father.

Hours seem to pass before he delivered his verdict.

"First of all, there *is* no older brother named Sunil in the family. Second of all, Rajesh Vanjare has asked his parents to take his name out of the matrimonial columns."

Mrs Bastikar frowned. "And why is that?"

"Because he's got himself engaged to a Swedish nurse."

The words cut like a knife. Monisha clutched her chest. Mrs Bastikar stared anxiously at her daughter.

"Just heartburn," shouted Monisha as she ran up the stairs, fighting back tears.

As if it wasn't bad enough being conned by a petty criminal and his Oscar-winning performance. The best candidate on her mother's shortlist had fallen prey to an unbeatable competitor.

A stunning, blonde nurse.

Thud. Thud. The panic began again. She was several days into her trip, but no closer to meeting the man she would marry. And now she was beginning to wonder whether it would ever happen at all.

5

The previous day's events had rattled everybody. Aunt Romila wished she'd been around. She could spot a conman a mile away. Uncle Shyam called Leela Bastikar an 'idiot' and made her install a security camera. Uncle Rohit told her to get the 'maple syrup' out of her brain, for she was far too sweet and trusting. And now, each time the phone rang, Monisha and her mother were a bag of nerves.

So, when it was proposed that all introductions should take place with Mrs Bastikar's siblings present, Monisha nodded acquiescently. Even though, by having to co-ordinate diaries, the whole process would take longer.

When she heard that the next suitor would be attending with his parents in two days' time, finally it seemed that things were looking up. She would even be allowed to sit in. No more being tucked away in her room or hiding behind chests. Uncle Shyam and Aunt Romila would be there for moral support. And, now the weather was hotting up, instead of tea and samosas there would be street snacks and mouth-watering cold drinks. Mmm!

When the time came, the helper stood by the door, while the others waited in the lounge room. Uncle Shyam kept his eyes fixed on the cricket. Leela Bastikar and Aunt Romila fussed over the cushions. Monisha sat in an armchair with her head buried in a gossip magazine. Each time she heard a passing car, she almost jumped out of her skin.

Finally, when the Meru family appeared on camera, the helper giggled. As they entered, Leela Bastikar stood dumbstruck for a few seconds before she welcomed them in. Uncle Shyam said a brief namaste and turned back towards the cricket. Aunt Romila appeared worried. Monisha's heart instantly sank to the floor.

Each one of them was massive. Three times her size at least.

Roly-poly, red-faced and pouring with sweat they waddled towards the sofas and sat down, barely leaving space for Monisha's family. For the next hour, she watched with horror as Mr and Mrs Meru, and their son Nimal, guzzled down the street snacks and dripped sweat all over the glass coffee table. Every five minutes she glanced hopefully at the clock, praying that the torture would end.

Uncle Shyam sensed her desperation. "I think at this point, we should leave it to Monisha and Nimal as to whether they want to take things further," he said, in a booming voice. "After all they are *big* enough now."

The place erupted with laughter when they'd left. Uncle Shyam couldn't understand how Nimal Meru had made it into the shortlist.

Aunt Romila threw her arms up in the air. "How do you expect us to know? The advertisement didn't say he was the size of an elephant!"

Monisha hadn't found it funny. Her mind flashed back to the conversation she'd had with Tina at Café Uno. Right now, falling in love seemed a far better option. Arranged marriage was fast becoming a freak show, played out by snobby in-laws, men with lisps, con artists, fat men and men who'd secretly got engaged. It was getting tiresome, the repetitive sequence that began with fear and fried food, and ended with heartburn and disappointment. She was beyond tears now.

When Uncle Shyam and Aunt Romila left, the place felt empty. It was time for dinner now. An entire day had passed. Monisha let out a heavy sigh as the helper carried in a steaming pot of rice.

"Do you have the number of a travel agent, Mom?" she asked after some time.

Leela Bastikar began spooning out lentils. The creases on her forehead thickened deeply.

"Whatever for?"

Monisha mixed the rice with the lentils and slowly lifted a forkful into her mouth. She could taste nothing.

"I want to change my ticket… Maybe I'll spend a few days with Dad before heading off to Boston."

Mrs Bastikar sent the helper to water the plants in the garden. He was a notorious gossip. She was certain that the whole street knew that she'd handed over a fistful of money to a con artist.

"Please stay a little longer Monisha," she said when he'd gone. "I've been here for six weeks, clearing out this house, reading the columns, consulting astrologers, making phone calls. Remember, this is harder on me than it is on you." Her voice trailed off. She swallowed. "Because when it's all over, I lose you to somebody else."

Ugh! The familiar tune of her mother's emotional blackmail. This time she was not quite ready to succumb. Monisha ate the rest of her meal in silence.

When the phone rang an hour later, her mother was in the shower and the helper in the garden. Monisha let it ring several times before she decided to pick up.

"Hello, I'm Shailesh Kulkarni," said a gentleman, in a deep voice, which bore only traces of an Indian accent. "Am I still okay to visit tomorrow morning?"

"Have you made an appointment?", she asked.

Leela Bastikar ignored her arthritic pains and scuttled down the staircase in her bathrobe. Instantly she snatched the phone out of Monisha's hands.

"Who is calling please?" she asked in the sugary voice reserved for prospective bridegrooms and their families.

"Yes, yes, tomorrow morning is fine. We know about the traffic in Andheri."

Monisha rolled her eyes.

"So, is he the father, the uncle, the cousin or the helper?"

Mrs Bastikar had never got to grips with sarcasm. She smiled sweetly.

"No, he is a thirty-one-year-old surgeon. Five-foot eleven-inches tall. And he is coming from Andheri, on a motorbike!"

"Great," said Monisha.

There'd be one more left after this one. And then the plane ride home.

6

The Mumbai suburbs of Andheri East and Juhu were only a few miles apart. After hitting Swami Vivekananda Road, the journey took less than twenty minutes. But the city was rarely free of traffic jams. On a bad day, the trip could last two hours. Fortunately for Shailesh Kulkarni, that Sunday morning the highways were deserted. So, he was able to glide into Sitara Road at half past ten sharp, with his hair still smooth and his countenance unruffled.

He greeted Leela Bastikar, Aunt Romila, Uncle Shyam and Uncle Rohit with individual namastes, and then removed his shoes. Neatly, beside them, he placed his helmet. When Mrs Bastikar ushered him into the lounge room, he waited for the seniors to take their places first. Before he sat down, he glanced over at Monisha and nodded.

She caught a glimpse of his hair, full and thick; it fell in neat waves round his ears. He was tall and solidly built, with rich, chocolaty skin. She watched him pick up a single coconut sweet and chew on it thoughtfully. He took a sip of the iced water offered to him and thanked the helper. A chill ran through her spine. Could he be the one?

There were five other people present. Monisha had to stop herself from staring. She'd never hear the end of it if they caught her. Upstairs in her room she had felt isolated. Here, she was completely exposed. Right now, she wished she was tucked away safe, behind the chest on the landing. A flush of heat burned her cheeks. She was red! Hot and red! She hoped no one would notice.

Uncle Shyam broke the ice and asked Shailesh Kulkarni about his family. Her ears pricked up. Where were they? He told them that he shared an apartment with his widowed mother. Apparently, she was an easy-going lady who didn't interfere in his daily affairs. He had only one sister, and she was planning a move to Dubai with her husband.

Monisha looked down at her lap and suppressed a smile. So far, so good. The next round of questions about his education and career came from Uncle Rohit. In the same sombre voice, she recalled hearing on the phone, Shailesh Kulkarni traced his journey from a hill-station primary school through to medical school in Karnataka.

"I finished my surgical training in Mumbai. The practice is starting to pick up here," he said. "But I have been offered a fellowship in New York. It would be a shame to waste the opportunity."

Monisha's jaw dropped. New York! This was the best bit of news she'd heard so far. Here he was, the Brahmin doctor from Mumbai she'd dreamed of! Taller, older and darker than her. And with a job in New York, he'd only be a few hours away. They could catch up on weekends. There was no family to get past either! Just an easy-going mother-in-law and a sister-in-law abroad. She waited with bated breath, hungry to hear more.

Shailesh Kulkarni studied the clock. "I'd better head off now," he said. "A friend of mine is in town. My mother has invited him for lunch and she always cooks a feast."

The others rose after him. Leela Bastikar began fussing.

"What about tea… or coffee?"

He said he didn't drink either. Leela Bastikar protested.

"But you ate nothing here!"

Monisha cringed at the irony. The other contenders had gulped down expensive teas and freshly made street food, and here was the man she most wanted to impress.

"I don't really snack between meals. It's an unhealthy Indian habit," he laughed.

Well handled, she thought. Assertive, but not offensive. And he was health conscious as well!

Shailesh Kulkarni made his way towards the door, picked up his helmet and turned back to wave goodbye.

"Okay then," he said with a slight twist of his head.

Oh God! Their meeting was over. He hadn't asked her a single question or suggested going on a date. No 'see you later' either.

And what the hell was 'Okay then!' supposed to mean?

The thunderous roar of a motorcycle engine blasted her eardrums, then the harsh scrape of wheels along the dirt. He was gone.

Leela Bastikar beamed.

"I really like him. I like the sound of his voice."

Monisha glowered back. Couldn't she see that it was all going to end in the same way, with emptiness and dashed hopes?

"So," asked Aunt Romila, "how is his mother going to manage on her own when he moves to America?"

But Monisha didn't hear the question, nor was she interested in any of the discussion taking place. She darted up to her bedroom and began gathering her things. Unfortunately, the travel agents were closed on a Sunday. First thing on Monday, she would head over to one and change her ticket.

The phone rang. It was Aunt Romila's daughter Riya, asking her if she'd like to see a movie and if so, a tear-jerker or a comedy. Monisha took up the offer gladly and chose the tear-jerker. She was in no mood for jokes.

That afternoon, the two girls wandered through the mall, with Riya pointing out various couples and sniggering.

"Look at him with his soccer-ball belly! Do you think his wife is overfeeding him, to give him a heart attack so she can have his money?"

For the first time in days, Monisha began laughing. Over cold coffee and swirls of gooey chocolate ice cream, the girls reminisced about their childhood capers at Sitara Road. Rescuing lizards, climbing mango trees and outdoor baths in a bucket. At the cinema, they wept and blubbered over the film, which was about a blind girl and her lost love.

It was dark when she got in. Her mother greeted her, flapping about like an excitable bird. Shailesh Kulkarni had called back when she was out. He wanted to meet her for coffee.

There was a stunned silence. Monisha digested the words.

"He offered you a ride on his motorbike, but Uncle Shyam thought it wouldn't be right. So, he'll send his car; that is, if you say "yes.""

Monisha felt her mother's eyes glaring.

"Yes," she said, so quietly that she had to repeat herself. "Tell him yes."

7

Dressing for a coffee date with a prospective husband proved rather difficult for Monisha. Traditional clothes might seem old-fashioned. A skirt would be too western. After much deliberation, she settled on a white salwar suit, with tight leggings. She draped a pale organza scarf round her shoulders and dusted her lips with shimmery gloss. She smiled at herself in the mirror. There! She'd nailed it: a perfect blend of East and West.

Mrs Bastikar barged in for a last-minute inspection. After completing a head-to-toe survey, she gently lifted the scarf from her daughter's shoulders and turned it into a veil. "Oh my!" she cried. "Just like an Indian bride".

Outside, Uncle Shyam sounded his horn loudly. Monisha made her way nervously through the front door and into the courtyard. Thoughts buzzed round her head. If this coffee date didn't work out, there was only one man left to meet. And if that didn't work out, she'd be returning home. Single. Gulp!

Leatherhead Café was teeming with backpackers; tattoos, nose rings and harem pants abounded. Giant photographs of Elvis Presley adorned its mauve walls. Skinny, blonde girls and pony-tailed men leaned at the counter. At a table by the window sat Shailesh Kulkarni, slouched behind a frothy glass of beer. Monisha took a deep breath and walked over.

He offered to buy her a beer. She agreed to a weak shandy. It took a while to arrive.

"You don't drink?"

She shook her head and sipped cautiously.

"It's only eleven o'clock."

Shailesh shrugged his shoulders.

"And hot... I hate these interviews. How many have you said no to?"

"A couple," she replied, staring into her drink. She didn't wish to elaborate further and be reminded of the con artists, snobs and no-shows.

He changed the subject.

"What do you like to do in your spare time?"

"I learned classical dance," said Monisha, thinking back to Mrs Bhatia's classes. What was the answer he'd like to hear? She hesitated.

"And I cook."

Shailesh Kulkarni raised his eyebrows, in disbelief.

"What? No parties or nightclubs?"

Her heart began thumping rapidly. He must think she was a complete prude.

"Been to one or two," she said. Scenes flashed through her mind of girls keeled over in doorways, vomiting.

"They start off fun, and then somebody gets their drink spiked and ends up in the emergency room."

Shailesh Kulkarni began laughing.

"Sounds like quite an adventure... so you were the good Indian girl: staying at home and rolling chapattis, then?"

Monisha huffed, loudly. All those dinner parties, just to preserve herself for someone like Shailesh Kulkarni and now she was being ridiculed.

"Yes, I stayed in on Saturday nights... and avoided date rape."

Suddenly a dark shadow crept over him. The smile left his face. A waiter brought over a pint of Guinness and passed it towards him. Shailesh skimmed the foam off the top and began licking it off the sides.

"I'm only teasing. I prefer it that way. Have you ever... had a boyfriend?"

She breathed a sigh of relief.

"No. Have you ever—"

He cut her off before she could finish. Noticing her shandy glass was empty, he called the waiter back.

"Nothing serious, I wouldn't be here otherwise."

As they waited, Shailesh Kulkarni eyed her up a little more closely. He observed that her organza scarf was trailing along the floor and picked it up. Monisha thanked him. Now it smelled of cigarette ash and was covered in flecks of sawdust.

"You did well to get into Boston. What do you want to do eventually?"

"Oncology," said Monisha, brushing the dirt away. Somehow it didn't sound quite enough on its own.

"Research as well," she added. Even though she had no clue how she'd squeeze that in between marriage and kids, and medical board exams.

He nodded, but seemed less than impressed.

"I'll be doing research in New York, with Professor Sawhney. He was from my med school… made it big. The pancreas is his thing."

It all sounded very exciting, but there was one burning question. Monisha leaned forward. Why hadn't he applied for surgical residency?

Shailesh Kulkarni stopped for a minute and stared down at the table.

"My scores were good: high 230s. But I wanted a break…" He looked into her eyes. "It's been so crazy, with surgical training, charity work, Indian exams and US exams. Now starting up the practice."

He pulled his chair closer towards her.

"I really want to spend time on other things now."

She felt him. Close. The beer on his breath. His new leather shoes. Thoughts catapulted through her mind: seeing Times Square and Central Park together and slurping on clam chowder.

Oh! She crossed her legs. Squeezed them tight.

The fan wobbled clumsily above them. Lost in her thoughts, it was some time, before Monisha noticed that he'd began speaking again.

"My father died when I was in medical school. Cancer."

His eyes glazed over as the scenes came charging back, one by one. He shook his head; the soft waves of hair were now moistened with sweat and clinging to his head. Monisha sat up, straight as a tack.

"Everything changed overnight. The hospital bills were huge. My mother took up work in a factory… sewing."

He continued shaking his head from side to side, as if he were shaking the memories out.

Suddenly his face broke into an impulsive smile and he began to nod thoughtfully. "Finally, things are looking up!" he said, with his eyes shining. "My practice is expanding… I was accepted in New York." He paused and stared straight at her. "And now I've met you."

Monisha blushed and smiled back. Her heart flew into a wild flutter. He was the one for her, she knew it. Oh God, he felt the same! And here they were, amongst a sea of Dutch hippies, sitting at this cracked wooden table, breathing in the stench of beer and unwashed clothing, with sawdust and cigarette ash on the floor beneath them. Two people who realised they were perfect for each other. What a strange and wonderful place it was, the Leatherhead Café!

Shailesh sipped the rest of his Guinness quietly. The waiter arrived with a lemonade for her. In a flash, his expression changed and his voice seethed with bitterness. "They do some kind of personal check now, dig up the dirt; you know, speak to professors… ex-girlfriends." He rolled his eyebrows and began tapping the table with each of his fingers, making an odd unsynchronised noise. "One of your uncles is probably on the phone to my medical college right now."

It was almost lunch time, and city workers were slowly drifting in. The crowd was beginning to swell, so Shailesh Kulkarni had to shout to get himself heard.

"Then there's the bogus astrological consultation. The man tells you what you want to hear and sends you a large bill!"

"Really?" she enquired. "I don't know much about these things."

He frowned and looked at his watch; there were a couple of hernias waiting. Would she mind assisting? They could grab some food at another place, in a couple of hours or so. Monisha nodded. She had nothing better to do. But he was adamant. She would have to ask permission from her family first.

"I don't want to be accused of stealing you away."

Leela Bastikar was delighted when she heard. So much so that she completely forgot that her daughter would be straddled on a motorbike, behind a man she'd only just met. And if Uncle Shyam saw them, there'd be trouble.

"Of course, Monisha!" she screeched at the top of her lungs.

"Of course, you must go."

8

Sitara Road was at its calmest at six in the morning. Without the din of traffic, there were only gentle sounds. Crows cawing lazily. Rickshaws squeezing their rubber tyres along the path. The shuffle of slippers on gravel, as helpers arrived for work. Soon the noises would come from inside. A trickle of water from the tap. A tinkle when it filled the kettle.

As Monisha lay in bed waiting for the helper to bring in her tea, pleasant thoughts flitted round her head. With every passing day, her feelings for Shailesh Kulkarni were becoming stronger. Her family had unanimously agreed to cancel the final suitor. Now even they could see that there was no better match.

Things had started off awkwardly at the café. She hadn't appreciated his joke about the chapattis. And he'd seemed uncomfortable and embittered about the whole 'marriage' thing. But once he'd entered the hospital, Shailesh Kulkarni came to life.

Unlike the brash senior doctors, he treated nurses with respect. When the lift operator showed him a lump on his arm, he'd removed it that afternoon, free of charge. He'd performed the hernia repairs deftly, while she assisted.

"Everybody worships him," the theatre sister had whispered in her ear.

Later, she'd met some of his boisterous juniors. They shared their stories over pav bhaaji and masala tea: hilarious tales of mishaps and blunders. Dr Kulkarni was forever bailing them out of trouble. She noticed him blush.

Sipping cappuccinos, they'd discussed their favourite books and films. He loved Steve Mc Queen and *To Kill a Mockingbird*. So did she. He wanted children, but, with careers like theirs, he thought two were quite enough.

"A boy and a girl would be nice," she'd said.

"After we finish our training," was his reply.

He was just what she needed. Practical, sensible and caring. A tall, dark handsome surgeon, with a job lined up in New York. Monisha hugged the blankets tightly. A thrill shot through her body. She grinned from ear to ear. He was the one!

And she couldn't wait to tell Tina.

She wouldn't rub her nose in it or say something like 'I told you so'. She'd just present the facts, neatly and simply. Out of 'millions of strangers', her mother had shortlisted eight suitors. And, after some false starts, in the presence of her extended family, she had met her perfect match. Using precisely the same process that had been going on for thousands of years.

Three days later, in the courtyard of the Palamo Restaurant, their families came together. Eight of them, sandwiched underneath a giant umbrella. Aunt Romila, Uncle Shyam, Uncle Rohit, her mother and herself on one side; the Kulkarnis on the other. Laughing and chatting, slurping and clinking glasses of mango lassi. Tucking into plates of kebabs.

Monisha met her future sister-in-law, Ayesha, who was pale skinned and pretty, and the widowed Mrs Kulkarni, frail and bespectacled, dressed in traditional white. When they called her over to their side, to balance the table, everyone giggled at the meaning.

The excitement sent her rushing off to the toilet. Uncle Shyam followed her and gently took hold of her arm.

"Monisha, we usually make some checks before we go ahead."

She nodded hastily.

"University professors, colleagues…"

She sped towards the neon sign.

"Would you like us to—"

She cut him off when they reached the ladies' room.

"That won't be necessary, Uncle, but thanks anyway."

Uncle Shyam raised his eyebrows and opened his mouth as if to ask a question, but then stopped himself. His niece was an educated woman, she knew what she wanted. They were both doctors. What was the point of prying?

"I suppose… All we have to do now is fix a date."

She beamed.

The night before she flew back to Boston, Monisha Bastikar was engaged to Shailesh Kulkarni. The ceremony took place at the house in Sitara Road. Prayers were made at the family shrine. The couple exchanged rings and fed each other sweet vermicelli rice pudding in front of the gods. Confetti-filled balloons were burst open. Fire crackers zoomed and whirred above their heads.

And the smile she'd woken up with that morning never left her face for one moment. She'd found him at last, the husband she'd waited for all her life.

9

The alarm awoke Monisha with a jolt. It was half past five in the morning. The smell of garbage wafted in. Where was she? Not Sitara Road, not Adam Court. This was her flat in Northend, just across the road from that cruel, labyrinthine workhouse, St Anthony's. A sickly dread heaved through her. Twenty minutes to shower and eat. Fifteen if she didn't move now. Soon enough, Professor Folstein would be limping round the ER and firing off impossible questions.

She was three months in. Every day, the same grizzly cycle. Wake at half past five. Start seeing patients at six. Then, for the next fifteen hours, get buzzed, beeped, air-paged and quick-dialled. Each time, a different frantic voice: "Report to the nurse's station". "Report to the ER". "Report to the radiology department".

Report. Report. Report.

She was perpetually running in and out of the gloomy,

grey maze of buildings. Through vast, crowded walkways or eerily empty corridors. Down fire-escapes. Up lifts. Running to where the jobs lay waiting.

"Sign this... Take a look at him... Insert that... Write up those pills..."

When she'd finish one task, a snarling nurse would have her straight onto the next.

By nine o'clock in the evening she was back in the flat, completely drained. Wolfing down lukewarm, leftover takeaway. Flicking through the channels; news, comedy and drama, all blurring into one giant mishmash of words and pictures.

At around ten o'clock, she'd scan through the latest copy of the physician's bible: *The New England Journal.* A short while later, she'd be sprawled out on top of a drool-stained page, snoring. She'd shake herself awake, brush her teeth and start reading again. Then she'd sleep until the alarm rang.

All day she was surrounded by a monotonous bunch who only talked work. They lived it, breathed it and injected it into every sentence. Eating and sleeping were distractions that got in the way. Except for the odd Red Sox game or a rare night on the town, the residents mostly wandered round St Anthony's, shadowing their seniors and rote learning facts.

She shared the flat with a Mr Anaesthesiology and Miss OB-GYN. They were both unfriendly folks, who said hello and rushed to their rooms. Miss OB-GYN only used the place for storage because she stayed at her boyfriend's house. Mr Anaesthesiology barely spoke. Who could blame him? Seven nights on, then seven long days, back to back. When she heard the toilet flushing, it meant he was in.

After a while, the loneliness became intense; it hung over her like a black cloud. Only a letter or a phone call from Shailesh could kill the misery. When his sombre voice came through the crackly line or when she smelled the diesel fumes in his dusty letters, Monisha came alive.

There had been a letter each month, packed with news. Ayesha had moved in with her baby girl Seema, now eleven weeks old. Mrs Kulkarni was a doting grandmother. His practice was picking up speed. Several big operations had come his way.

But he never mentioned a date for the wedding or moving to New York. After the initial thrill of hearing his voice subsided, she would pin him down and ask him leading questions. His answers were sketchy. He hoped to get married 'at some point'. His research fellowship could start 'any time he wanted it to'. But when she pressed him further, he said he was busy and ended the call, leaving her plans full of gaping holes.

She filled the emptiness with pipe dreams. Together they walked arm in arm on manicured lawns, wearing couture, like the Kennedys. Shailesh, the dashing surgeon, and she with perfect hair and glossed lips. Two chocolate-skinned children skipped behind them clutching candy floss.

One evening, a phone call from her mother brought her swiftly back to reality. The sugary voice had disappeared. Now her words came through, stern and hard.

"I think the Kulkarnis want to delay things. They haven't mentioned this, but Ayesha and her husband have separated. That's why she is living with them. Has Shailesh told you?"

"No."

Monisha let out a heavy sigh. She was tired. Tired of work. Tired of takeaway and textbooks. Too tired to talk about this now.

"He hasn't?"

Her mother was digging. She should have been an archaeologist: she had such a knack for digging out stuff from the past and analysing it.

"I have to go, Mom. Promise I'll call you tomorrow."

Thwack! She was gone. But she'd left a trail of nagging thoughts whirring round her head. Now it was impossible to eat or read or sleep. How did she find out about Ayesha? What were the Kulkarnis playing at? If something terrible had happened, why weren't they telling her? She was going to be part of their family, wasn't she?

She got up, washed her face and picked up *The New England Journal*. It was no use. The same thoughts came back to haunt her. She had to ask him.

Her fingers pressed the numbers. It was half past eight in the morning in Mumbai. Monisha jumped, scared when she heard him. He seemed surprised by her call.

"Is everything okay?"

"With me it is. But what about you all?"

Her heart beat faster in anticipation.

"All fine here." His voice was cheery and light.

"Well, I heard that… er…" She hesitated. A costly silence ensued. She eventually mustered up the courage to continue. "I heard that Ayesha and her husband have separated, and you want to delay the wedding."

He replied with a thundering boom. "Who told you that? Has your mother been gossiping?"

Her own voice rose to a shriek. "Why can't you just tell me the truth?"

Bam! The thought that had been sitting on the sidelines was out mid-field.

He let out a sigh and told her that Ayesha's husband was in Dubai. She'd wanted her mother to help with the baby, so she'd come to stay.

"So they're not divorcing?"

In the background she could heard a baby screaming, then it quietened.

"Is that why you rang me, Monisha, to find out about Ayesha?"

Now the crackling noises were starting up. She'd have to shout. That meant Mr Anaesthesiology would be banging on her door any second. She told him she only wanted to find out a date for the wedding and when he'd be starting in New York.

The crackling faded, and his voice came through softly.

"The job's in Wichita now."

'WICHITA!' screamed Monisha. Mr Anaesthesiology began banging on the wall.

She lowered her voice. "What happened to New York?"

Apparently, Professor Sawhney had filled all the jobs there. But it didn't matter; he wasn't in a rush to leave Mumbai.

Ugh! It was impossible to argue. He'd said it at their very first meeting and it had flown right over her head. But, on their dates, they'd grown closer. And he'd made her feel that he wanted to be with her and that he couldn't wait to get married.

Now there were oceans between them. Even in Wichita he'd be miles away. She'd have to fly to Chicago first and waste hours in the layover. Her imagination ran wild. She saw planes grounded and crowds of desperate people stranded in the Thanksgiving rush. Shailesh would be one of them. It was all too much. She began to cry.

Shailesh spoke over her.

"My dear wife-to-be… we may not see each other often, but when we do we'll make up for it. Right?"

Monisha sighed. It would be awkward. They'd hardly see each other. And, even when they did, they'd have to swap on-calls and book out leave. Somehow just slot each other in.

He sensed her unease.

"My mother is trying to set the date for November."

Oh dear God! It was only April.

He began rambling on about timings and such. Before July was inconvenient. The flat needed repairs and the landlord was unavailable. From July to October was inauspicious, so the priests wouldn't even consider it. It would have to be November, at the very earliest.

His voice trailed off. The line beeped over and over, until eventually it cut out by itself.

Monisha buried her face in her hands. A husband in Wichita, after an eleven-month wait. Still, it had to be better than being alone.

10

It was thirty-two degrees Celsius outside. As usual, Mumbai airport was chock-a-block. Everywhere people were chattering, sipping cold coffee or picking through platefuls of food with plastic forks: potato-filled pancakes and onion pakoras, or Bombay chaat with tamarind sauce. Monisha stared greedily as she made her way past them. November had come slowly, now time would race away.

The city, with all its colours, dazzled in the mid-afternoon sun. Sea-greens, turquoises, fiery oranges and gentle mauves on turbans and saris, even on trucks. She breathed in the choking fumes to remind herself she was here. The unmistakable stench of sweat, urine, rotting rubbish and spices hit her at once. Phew! She was here alright.

Her mother had meticulously planned her itinerary. The first three days would be spent in Sitara Road, for beauty treatments and last-minute shopping. Then the wedding would take up four days. After that they'd head off to Goa for their honeymoon. Just herself and Shailesh.

After almost a year, she would finally see him in the flesh, feel his touch on her skin, watch his lips move as he spoke. No more crackly telephone conversations. A tingle ran up through her calves. From somewhere in the distance, she heard a familiar voice. It was her cousin Riya.

"Here comes the bride!"

Monisha ran up to greet them. Aunt Romila and Riya hugged her, giggling.

Leela Bastikar stood at a distance shielding the sun out of her eyes with one hand. Almost everything had been arranged now. She rattled off the list in her head: gold, gifts, food, flowers and priest. When Monisha walked towards her, she froze.

"Mom, are you okay?"

"She's not okay," blurted Aunt Romila. "Her daughter is getting married. God knows how I'll be when Riya goes."

"That's why I'll just do it," said Riya. "Without telling anyone."

Mrs Bastikar smiled pensively. She knew what was coming. The residency had created distance. Marriage meant remoteness. Hadn't she once jumped on a plane with a man she'd barely met while her mother and sister wept at the airport.

"All the time and effort you spend raising a daughter is for someone else's benefit," she huffed. "Like watering your neighbour's garden."

The ten-minute walk to the jeep was painfully silent. As soon as they were all seated, Aunt Romila threw her head back and broke the ice. "Shailesh's sister is in strife."

The driver started up the engine with a splutter, and they pulled slowly out of the car park. A couple of street kids clung to the windows hoping for loose change.

"Why?" asked Monisha, trying to ignore them.

Aunt Romila removed her sunglasses and shot her an inquisitive stare. She used formal language when she didn't want the driver listening in. "Weren't you made *aware*? Her husband is *cohabiting* with another woman. He's even changed religion to take on a second *spouse*."

Monisha gasped. She was shocked for Ayesha and slightly taken aback that Shailesh had not told her.

"No… I didn't know."

"He obviously didn't want any scandal to come out before the wedding," said Mrs Bastikar.

Monisha shook her head in disbelief. It was true, Riya said. Their cook's sister had worked for the Kulkarnis and she knew everything.

Monisha sat, dumbstruck. When she thought about it, each letter from Shailesh had been filled with minutiae. He told her which birds were outside his window and complained about the soaring price of onions. But he'd never mentioned his brother-in-law leaving. She tried shrugging it off.

"Perhaps he didn't tell you in case you changed your mind," said Riya, slapping her on the thigh. It stung.

A large bump in the road made them all jump. Suitcases flew up and down in the boot. In one of them was a gift for her mother-in-law, a large, glass vase. Everything was beginning to jangle her nerves.

Monisha glared at Riya, while rubbing her thigh.

"Why would I do that?"

"Because you've suddenly inherited a lot of baggage," whispered Aunt Romila.

"Baggage?"

It seemed a strange choice of words. They were talking about her sister-in-law, who would be incomeless if her husband refused to pay alimony. And he could do that now he was living in Dubai.

Monisha stared out of the window; scores of women lined the roadside. Raven haired, with sparkling white teeth. Each of their futures at the mercy of God and some man.

"Remember Ayesha has no qualifications," said Leela Bastikar. "Even if she gets a job, it won't pay enough. She's going to be dependent on you."

Monisha raised her eyebrows and grunted. She'd waited for this wedding for almost a year and she wasn't going to let anyone ruin it. But the whole thing seemed quite bizarre. Her mother had always said it was white men who got their wives pregnant and scarpered.

"I thought this kind of thing didn't happen here."

Riya burst out laughing and made a sweeping motion with her hands.

"You think you know India because you've eaten curries and learned Kathak dance?"

For a moment, Monisha's mind wandered back to Mrs Bhatia's classes. Years she'd spent twirling round hardwood floors in pretty costume, dreaming. Perhaps Riya was right. She had absolutely no clue about what happened here.

The jeep wound its way into Sitara Road. In place of their dilapidated holiday home stood a gleaming white structure and a new driveway, lined with bamboo poles and boxes of lights. Monisha clapped her hands excitedly. Butterflies flitted wildly round her stomach. This was all for her wedding, for the marquee. The beautiful marquee!

Monisha gradually made her way into the lounge room behind the others. It was hot. The ceiling fans whirred fruitlessly above their heads. Helpers brought iced water. The women wiped themselves down with damp towels. Monisha ignored the constant trickle of sweat and kept her eyes peeled on all the gifts.

Every corner was packed with presents: saris, draped neatly over wooden trays and enveloped in cellophane. Gaudy silks. Pale white cotton. Exquisite lacework. Clutch bags and purses. A wallet and golden cuff-links were also wrapped, in clear cellophane, for all to see.

A thrill shot through her.

"Are these for us?" she asked, beaming.

"No," said Leela Bastikar, "for your in-laws. And they have a new fridge, a new bed… all meant for you, but Ayesha will grab it now."

Monisha glowered with rage and put both hands firmly on her hips.

"Can you just stop it! First, she's baggage. Now she's a thief!"

Rivers of sweat poured down Leela Bastikar's face.

"Do you know anything about your sister-in-law?" she hissed. "Or her marriage?"

Monisha wanted to scream. Her voice rose to a holler. It didn't matter. The girl had been abandoned and now she'd had a baby. At least some compassion was required!

Aunt Romila interrupted. "Yes, and now Shailesh is

so attached, he doesn't want to leave Mumbai… until the child is at least two."

Monisha surveyed the glittering wedding items. Suddenly a sharp burst of anger jolted through her, then pricked and burned at her skin.

11

After a night spent tossing and turning, Monisha arranged to meet Shailesh at his flat in Andheri, even though she knew Swami Vivekananda Road would be gridlocked, her cab would crawl along at a snail's pace and the driver would keep the meter running. She was desperate to see Shailesh in the flesh and discuss all she'd heard. Could he have really hidden the truth? Her mother's burning question played over in her mind. How much did she know about her future sister-in-law? Come to think of it, how much did she know about Shailesh?

She could recognise his curly handwriting instantly and his sombre telephone voice. She was aware that he would be working as a clinical fellow in a place called Hutchinson, near Wichita, under a Dr Cray.

And that he was going to marry her at the Taj Mahal Palace Hotel, in three days' time.

After an hour-long, doubly expensive journey, the cab pulled up outside the Kulkarni's flat. Monisha made her way up the staircase, her sandals slapping against the concrete steps. Her heart raced. Slap. Slap. Three more. Her fingers trembled as she pressed the bell.

Slowly, the door opened. Monisha bowed her head low and touched the feet of the old lady. Mrs Kulkarni gave her blessing with a smile, then asked her to take a seat while she fetched iced lime water.

The reception room was tiny. Its drab, grey walls bore a picture of the deceased Mr Kulkarni. Around his neck hung a fresh jasmine garland and, on either side of him, framed embroidered roses. Monisha sat down, clutching the vase she'd brought over as a gift. She carefully studied the picture of Mr Kulkarni and the embroidered roses. It was amateurish, schoolgirl sewing.

Her future mother-in-law returned with a glass of water on a tray.

"Thank you, wife," she said, taking her gift. "Ayesha made the roses," she added, beaming.

Monisha nodded quietly. A motorbike roared outside. Her heart began fluttering. Gulp! It was Shailesh.

He shot up the stairs and barged in, oily sweat pouring off him in puddles. As he entered, Mrs Kulkarni wiped his face, handed him a glass of iced lime water and placed a tower of steaming rice on the dinner table. In one sweeping motion.

Monisha couldn't help smiling when she saw him. She had waited eleven months for this moment. Shailesh grinned sheepishly, then walked to the sink. He washed his hands down to his elbows, as a surgeon would scrub. He cast her another quick glance, before becoming distracted by the array of curries on the table.

"She really looks after me you know," he said, pointing at his mother.

Once more, Mrs Kulkarni beamed with pride. Monisha's smile instantly vanished. She declined Mrs Kulkarni's offer of lunch.

"There are things we need to discuss, Shailesh."

"Like what?"

He picked up some rice.

"Like Ayesha's situation."

He frowned. A spoonful went into his mouth.

"Are they divorced?" Monisha looked him in the eye. "How is she going to support herself now... and Seema?"

Shailesh concentrated on mixing his curry and rice. Time stood still. It was a while before her spoke. "Did your mother send you over here to ask?"

She could feel herself boiling up.

Mrs Kulkarni looked pleadingly at Monisha. Ayesha would be back soon. She'd done all the shopping, alone. It was mad out there, with the wedding season starting up. And the poor girl was exhausted! Surely, they could discuss this another time.

She was cut off mid-sentence by Shailesh. "Mother we might as well tell her everything if she's going to be part of the family."

The old lady sighed and eased herself into one of the screechy, wooden dining chairs. Her knees creaked. Shailesh stopped eating and stared vacantly at Monisha. An eerie silence descended across the room. He took in a deep breath.

"My sister was a beautiful girl. After my father's death, she went off the rails… Dropped out of university and fell head over heels in love with a gangster."

"It was my fault; I couldn't keep my eye on her," Mrs Kulkarni spluttered. "I was out trying to earn a living after their father died."

Shailesh recounted the story. He was in medical school, his mother was out sewing sheets and Ayesha was riding round ghettos with a criminal, when everyone thought she was in lectures. He paused.

"Then one night… she was gang raped."

Monisha sat bolt upright.

She'd learned her lesson all right, he said. He'd asked his lawyer friend to press charges, but nothing came of it, so they tried to marry her off. But by then she had a criminal record – and she'd been raped. Shailesh shook his head bitterly.

"No educated man from a decent family would want a wife like that. We were lucky enough to find Roshan."

Mrs Kulkarni took her glasses off and gently brushed away tears. "Most of my jewellery was sold to wipe off her criminal record. The rest went to Roshan as dowry. Then we came here to start afresh."

Monisha sat dumbstruck. The story got worse. Ayesha wasn't pregnant after the rape. The baby was Roshan's. And he'd known, before he'd upped and left.

Mrs Kulkarni placed her head in her hands. "Ayesha is under the spell of Saturn, but—" She stopped short when she heard the doorbell.

Within seconds, Ayesha was standing before them laden with carrier bags. Sweat streamed down her pale skin. Her hip-length plait had thinned. Her face was expressionless. She greeted the bride-to-be and ran to the child's room. When she found Seema fast asleep, she rushed over to her brother.

For the next half hour, Monisha watched with horror as Mrs Kulkarni and Ayesha fussed over their beloved Shailesh. Had he eaten enough? Would he like some more chicken? Was it all too spicy? Did he need a peppermint pill? Ugh!

When he left the table, Ayesha handed him a clean t-shirt and a pair of cotton pyjama trousers. Shailesh threw the shirt back at her.

"I wanted the blue one, not this one!"

As Ayesha ran off to get another shirt, his mother asked him what he'd like for supper.

Monisha rolled her eyes. In this tiny flat, it was as if Shailesh was king and the women were his subordinates; their job being only to fetch and carry. Oh dear God, would she be expected to do the same?

"Can't you get your own clothes Shailesh? Do you have some kind of disability?"

He frowned, irritated at the suggestion. Mrs Kulkarni intercepted. But he worked "sooo" hard at the hospital. Why should he have to do the cooking and cleaning as well?

Monisha glared at the frail widow. "Well, in the West, men and women work equally hard, and we all have to do the cooking and cleaning."

Her words came and went without acknowledgement, for the sound of Seema's spirited cries filled the air. She was a pretty baby, with a shock of curly black hair, just like her uncle. While Mrs Kulkarni and Ayesha ate their lunch, Shailesh took the child into his room and asked her to join them.

Monisha pulled out a soft toy from her handbag and handed it to Seema. The crying gradually faded. She lifted her gently, inhaling the soothing smells of talcum powder and coconut oil. Then she imagined cradling her own baby in her arms.

Shailesh watched them both. "Not long now before our big day."

Monisha smiled and nodded. The baby gurgled.

"I can't wait," he added with a twinkle in his eye.

She melted. This was the Shailesh she remembered from before.

"You're going to be part of the family now."

Thump! Thump! Her heart started to race. She pushed herself closer to him, so their legs were touching. She raised her hand towards his face, ready to run her fingers through his curls. Stainless-steel plates clanged in the kitchen. Water gushed from a tap.

He pulled away.

"I think it's best if you spend the next couple of days with my mother and Ayesha. I'll be at work, but I can send you home in the evening."

Her arms and legs felt numb.

He thought it would be best, never mind what she wanted.

She told him her mother needed her at home, and that there was shopping to finish.

He shook his head, then lowered it.

"This is more important. My mother could even teach you a few recipes."

The pin-drop silence that ensued was broken when the phone rang. It was Aunt Romila. The jeep was on its way. Monisha breathed a sigh of relief and gathered her things.

12

The following morning, the house on Sitara Road was heaving. Outside the marquee was being strewn with leaves. The wires for the chandeliers were almost threaded. Mediterranean fan palms and potted roses were arriving in boxes. Gardeners trudged round carrying hose pipes and giant watering cans. Inside, the helpers ran about in a frenzy. Hot oil sizzled and splattered in the kitchen, and the scent of coriander oozed its way out, through the sitting room and towards the hallway. At the dining table, Professor Bastikar tucked into a giant omelette. Aunt Romila and Riya flicked through the newspapers, while Monisha sat with her head in her hands.

"Shailesh wants me to spend the day with his mother and sister rather than out shopping," she sighed.

"Of course he does," said Aunt Romila, biting into a piece of toast and sipping her black tea. "He wants you to get used to living with them."

Monisha gulped, then swallowed. How could everything have changed so quickly? When she'd first met Shailesh, Ayesha was moving to Dubai with her husband.

"I didn't think it would end up like this."

Aunt Romila burst out laughing. Crumbs flew everywhere. "None of us do!"

A helper arrived with a plate of crushed chillies. Leela Bastikar sprinkled a spoonful over her omelette. "I knew that his mother would have to stay with Shailesh. But not Ayesha… stupid girl."

"Very stupid," echoed Aunt Romila.

So they knew about Ayesha's misadventures! Monisha shifted uncomfortably in her chair. It made sense now, their complete lack of sympathy and how in their eyes she'd amounted to little more than 'baggage'.

Riya lifted her head from her newspaper and stared thoughtfully at her cousin and Aunt Leela. If she were the one getting married, she told them, she'd keep out of the way of her in-laws and hit the shops.

Leela Bastikar frowned. "Marriage is about compromise," she said before turning towards her daughter. "We won't give you up to the Kulkarnis for the entire day, Monisha, maybe from three till seven."

Monisha did the sums in her head. Two hours alone with her in-laws and two with Shailesh present. Give or take. Ugh! It seemed an awfully long time.

But Aunt Romila thought it was a perfectly good suggestion. That way, they'd get to finish the shopping and squeeze in an afternoon nap.

"While you natter with your mother-in-law!" added Riya, slapping Monisha on the thigh.

Monisha put on a brave face and rubbed her thigh. Riya's slaps always hurt, but her mouth hurt more than her hand.

"Anyway, Shailesh wants me to learn some of her recipes," she said sheepishly.

Suddenly a spoon shook, rattled and spun onto the floor. A cup clunked noisily against a saucer. Her mother shot her the most fearsome glare. "You already know how to cook, Monisha… I TAUGHT YOU."

A deathly silence followed, interrupted only by the slurping of tea. Professor Bastikar cleared his throat. "Oh Leela, just think when Swanker marries, he may want to eat some things that you make."

Leela Bastikar frowned so deeply that the lines on her forehead appeared in triplicate. She rose swiftly, leaving her omelette untouched. Within seconds she'd reached the staircase. She struggled up, one step at a time, until her voice reverberated from the landing.

"MAKE SURE HE HAS YOU HOME FOR DINNER."

As everyone else left the table, the helpers carried on past, pretending not to have heard a thing.

For the next four hours Aunt Romila's jeep trundled merrily between bumpy roads and air-conditioned shopping malls. The ladies giggled as Riya paraded round with lacy lingerie slipped over her clothes. "Am I gorgeous, Shailesh? Don't you just want to eat me?" she repeated as she twirled.

Monisha watched with awe as thick bundles of cash were handed over to shop assistants in return for bags piled with a ridiculous amount of clothing. There was beachwear, travel-wear, honeymoon-wear, day salwar suits and night saris. How could a bride need so much?

"Enjoy it while you can," said Aunt Romila. "Before the thorns begin to prick."

At precisely half past two, the jeep thudded to a halt in front of the gleaming white house. Her mother, Aunt Romila and Riya jumped out, clutching bags and boxes. A pain shot through her. It had already started. Any minute now, the drab, grey walls. Prick. Ayesha's blank face. Prick. Mrs Kulkarni's widow's sari. Prick. The potted roses studding the courtyard disappeared in a blur of pink and red tears.

It was Ayesha who answered the door, puffy-eyed, having just woken. In the reception room, sari blouses were stacked high on a chair. Loose threads dangled everywhere. A sewing machine clattered in the background. "I'll take over mother," she said, nodding a quick hello and picking up a few blouses.

The clattering stopped. Mrs Kulkarni hobbled towards them.

"You couldn't have come sooner? I've spent all morning roasting and grinding spices"

Monisha turned her head and rolled her eyes. Yikes! Ayesha had caught her. Her cheeks began to burn.

"She won't have *all* morning to roast and grind spices mother, she's a doctor."

Mrs Kulkarni pouted.

"But it's for the mutton curry… his favourite."

Monisha walked briskly towards the kitchen. It was too late. Ayesha's eyebrows were raised. Surely she'd tell Shailesh! Her mother's voice rang out. Marriage is compromise. She took a deep breath and lowered her head. C-o-m-p-r-o-m-i-s-e.

"Your mother is right. I must learn to make it."

Job done. Mrs Kulkarni grinned from ear to ear. Ayesha busied herself with the sari blouses. The baby snored contentedly.

Monisha jotted down the list of ingredients as Mrs Kulkarni called them out: green cardamom; nutmeg one-quarter; cinnamon stalks times four; roasted cumin seeds; whole coriander seeds; whole black pepper; and seven large cloves of garlic. She flinched and added room freshener, breath freshener and perfume to her list.

For the next hour, they marinated and basted in silence. The vegetable curries were less trouble. No onions or garlic to rouse the senses, for Hindu widows were forbidden from eating such ingredients. The scent of spices wafted through the tiny kitchen into the room where Ayesha sewed, and onto the blouses. Monisha tiptoed across so as not to wake the baby.

"Are these for yourselves?" she asked.

"Heavens no! We have to earn our keep," replied Ayesha, with a mouthful of pins.

"Does it pay?"

Ayesha immediately stopped pinning and looked up. Blouses and repairs didn't, but proper sewing did. And she'd learn one day. Her eyes shone with hope. For once.

"In the States, a lot of people take night classes," said Monisha.

Ayesha's half-smile disappeared and the blankness returned. She began gathering up the unfinished garments and stuffing them into a sack. As she opened the shutters, a stream of light shot through the window. Swirls of dust particles bobbed and danced.

Seema began to scream. Ayesha was going to make tea, Monisha offered to do it instead. On a shelf in the kitchen, she found a jar filled with loose tea leaves. She tossed three spoonfuls into a pan of boiling water and waited for the delicate aroma to fill the air, like when the helper made tea at Sitara Road. But it was a horrible, woody smell that blasted through her nostrils. She screwed up her face.

A voice came from behind, loud and booming.

"Busy in the kitchen already. What have you made?"

It was Shailesh. Mrs Kulkarni handed him a glass of iced lime water.

"Only tea," she said, smiling. Disappointment was etched across his face.

The baby toddled towards him excitedly. Ayesha switched on the TV. Shailesh climbed onto the bed holding the child. He motioned for Monisha to sit. But, before she could, Mrs Kulkarni and Ayesha clambered up.

Trumpets blasted the news theme. A chilly breeze drifted in. Monisha squeezed herself into a corner and began watching. But the language was more complicated than in Hindi class; she couldn't follow a word. And the comedy show afterwards went completely over her head. Actors yelled at one other in absurd, falsetto voices while the Kulkarnis wobbled about in fits of laughter.

Aargh! Monisha winced in pain. Leg cramp. She scrambled up and made for the door, taking deep breaths and rubbing her leg. The tightness went.

Shailesh walked over to her side.

"Are you okay?", he asked.

No, she wasn't okay. How could she be? She'd waited almost a year to marry this man. Thoughts pricked away at her flesh. He'd been so taken with her when they'd first met. Prick. But now, with Ayesha and Seema in tow, she didn't matter as much. Prick. And to the Kulkarni women she was just an interloper. Prick. An intruder who threatened to take away their king. Prick. She fought back tears.

"I have to get home."

Home. Where was that? Twenty-three Adam Court, Burlington or the apartment she shared with Miss OB-GYN and Mr Anaesthesiology, who were never there? Or Sitara Road, Juhu, with Riya's thigh slapping and Aunt Romila's snide comments.

Shailesh took her hand. "Come. I'll take you. Why don't we grab a drink first?"

A lone tear trickled down her face. She lowered her head further, so he wouldn't see.

"And some time alone," he whispered. His breath felt hot on her neck.

Mrs Kulkarni rose from the bed, glanced at Monisha's lowered head and then shifted her eyes towards her son.

"What's wrong?" she enquired.

Shailesh dropped Monisha's hand like a hot potato.

"Just cramp," he replied, before dashing off to find a jacket.

Minutes later they were soaring down Swami Vivekananda Road on his motorbike. The word 'BAR' flashed before them, then a string of lights strewn round a tree. They stopped. The place stank of urine.

He ushered her to the back and ordered a beer. They found a quiet corner. He pulled his chair closer towards hers. The old Shailesh returned. She felt her knees weakening. She took a deep breath in and held her nose.

"I hoped we would build our own life, Shailesh."

He stared into the distance and took a sip.

"We will, in time."

"But Ayesha?"

He told her she wanted to open her own business, right here in Mumbai. Monisha tried to suppress a smile. Perhaps things were not going to be quite so bad after all.

13

It was the morning before the wedding, and the gifts from the groom's family were due any minute. Mrs Bastikar, Aunt Romila and Riya stood in the doorway, together with the wives and daughters of Uncle Rohit and Uncle Shyam. Excitement loomed all round. Eventually a car strewn with marigolds pulled up outside the gates. The women shrieked, and Riya let out an ear-piercing wolf whistle.

The groom's messenger, a cousin of Shailesh's, solemnly stepped out of the car. He greeted his audience with a namaste, then proceeded towards the car boot. Intimidated by all the attention, he fumbled with the lock. On the third attempt, it opened, and he pulled out several gift baskets. One by one he carried them into the house. After he finished, the women swarmed round him. He declined their offers of food and drink, and fought his way back towards the door.

Leela Bastikar had not stopped smiling all morning, but when she discovered the photographer and videographer deeply engrossed in the cricket, she exploded with rage. "I HAVEN'T HIRED YOU TO WATCH TELEVISION!" she hissed as she marched the two men out of the sitting room.

On her way, she noticed Shailesh's cousin standing red-faced in the hallway. Instantly her sugary voice returned. "Would you mind bringing in the gifts again, dear boy?" she asked him. "For the cameramen?"

The groom's messenger reluctantly delivered the encore. When it was over he hurried back towards his car and ordered the driver to put his foot down. They sped off.

Monisha had witnessed all the commotion from behind the wooden chest on the landing. Now there was complete calm. All the women in the room quietly hovered over the baskets while the videographer filmed them. When she heard her name being called, she checked herself in the mirror and scurried down to open her gifts, with her pulse racing.

The first basket contained a jewellery box. Monisha eased off the cellophane. The velvet cover felt soft in her hands. Thwack, she opened the case. It contained a thin rope chain. Gold, at least. Aunt Romila briefly surveyed the baskets herself.

"That looks like it for jewellery", she remarked. "No earrings or bangles."

"Well, it would be silly for him to send it all by car," retorted Mrs Bastikar.

Monisha nodded. Perhaps Shailesh was being cautious. Either that or there was no more jewellery. The thought nagged her a little, but she shrugged it off and moved on to the other gifts.

The next two baskets were labelled 'Aunts' and 'Cousins'. Monisha pulled off the wrapping paper. Several silk saris tumbled onto the floor: blue, green, pink, red and mustard. Uncle Shyam's wife picked one up and ran her fingers through it. She screwed up her nose.

"Cheap," she said, "feels like a sack."

Monisha frowned. Images flickered through her mind: Ayesha, leaving her precious baby and wandering through shopping malls; buying gifts for her brother's wedding, when her own marriage had just ended. So painfully awkward. She glared at Uncle Shyam's wife.

Aunt Romila hastily passed her over another basket. This time the tag said 'Bride – lunch reception'. She tore open the cellophane. The women gasped when they caught sight of the sari. Monisha lowered her head to avoid their faces.

"What an awful colour combination!" screeched Uncle Rohit's wife. "Purple and bright green? What was Ayesha thinking?"

"It's obvious," said Riya, slapping her on the thigh. "She was thinking about an aubergine… in a forest!"

Uproarious laughter followed. Grunting and snorting echoed throughout the hallway. Monisha flushed with embarrassment. Anger surged through her body, and burned hot on her neck and face. She scrambled up off the floor.

"OH, FOR CRYING OUT LOUD!"

Monisha made for the stairs, kicking away crumpled bits of cellophane as she went. Soon she was safely in her bedroom, sitting on her bed.

Mrs Bastikar shot off behind her. Knee pains and hip pains were instantly forgotten. With adrenaline-charged footsteps she climbed the stairs. Within seconds she'd made it into the bedroom.

"You're taking things far too seriously, Monisha," she said, between breaths and after she'd pulled the door shut softly. "They're all joking with you."

The ceiling fan whirled wildly above them. Monisha sat hugging her pillow. Tears choked her throat.

"They're not joking, Mother. They're laughing at me!"

Mrs Bastikar shook her head. "Nonsense! This is all just fun. My cousins did exactly the same to me when I opened your father's gifts."

Monisha heaved a deep sigh. What was Ayesha thinking? Was purple and green a deliberate choice to make her look bad? Surely not.

There was a loud knock at the door. It was Aunt Romila, asking to be let in.

"NO!" cried Monisha.

"I've told Riya off!" her aunt pleaded. "She's grounded."

Monisha turned towards her mother in protest. Riya's groundings did absolutely nothing to control what came out of her spiteful tongue. She didn't want to see Aunt Romila now, and she didn't want to open any more gifts.

"And I don't want to look like an aubergine in a forest at the lunch reception!", she howled.

Which was precisely why she needed Aunt Romila, her mother explained. For when it came to arranging weddings, Aunt Romila had more experience than anyone.

Monisha groaned as she rose to unlock the door. Aunt

Romila crept in and found herself a corner on the bed. Leela Bastikar explained the dilemma.

Aunt Romila listened attentively. It was simple; Monisha had to tell her in-laws that she didn't want to wear the sari, without hurting their feelings. She paused to think. Perhaps she could say that everything else was lovely, but this one particular sari didn't suit her colouring. Would they mind if she chose another?

"Shall I ring them now?" asked Monisha, feeling slightly relieved.

Aunt Romila cringed and shook her head. This sort of thing was always done better in person. She'd have to ask the driver if he was free to take her over.

Monisha raced out of the door.

"But have your lunch before you leave," called her mother. "AND YOU MUST BE BACK BEFORE DUSK BECAUSE—"

"BECAUSE IT'S BAD LUCK, I KNOW!" shouted Monisha from the bottom of the stairs.

Aunt Romila rose from the bed and examined her sister quizzically.

"Do you think Shailesh is making much money?"

Leela Bastikar hurriedly straightened out the bedding and picked up loose threads and pieces of cellophane off the floor.

"I think he was doing well, until Ayesha and Seema turned up."

Aunt Romila nodded, as if she were in a trance. "Perhaps", she added, after some time.

In the sitting room, the rest of the baskets were opened gradually. Small things only. A tan leather handbag and matching coin purse. Pink lipstick and blusher. Gold sandals. Inexpensive, but tasteful.

The scent of rose petals and chicken biryani filled the air. The ladies made their way to the mahogany dining table. All was forgiven as they wolfed down their festive lunch. There were claps and cheers, and clay pots of pistachio ice cream. Then, a helper came over and whispered in Monisha's ear. Her heart began to beat faster.

Aunt Romila's driver tooted the horn four times. Monisha rose and washed her hands. She bid everyone goodbye. Aunt Romila and Mrs Bastikar watched from the doorway as she walked over to the jeep, with slow, hesitant footsteps. There was still one hurdle to cross.

14

As soon as Monisha set foot in the flat, Mrs Kulkarni welcomed her with smiles and open arms. Ayesha and Seema came running over to greet her. Her heart fluttered wildly, then butterflies became pangs of guilt. Surely she could have compromised on one sari!

"Did you get all our presents?" asked Ayesha. Excitement shone in her eyes.

Monisha avoided her gaze and nodded.

"So, did they like them?"

"Yes," she replied feebly.

Outside an engine purred. A couple of men chattered away, their voices muffled. She peered out of the window. It was the car strewn with marigolds. The groom's messenger climbed out first. Then Shailesh. Swoosh! The fluttering began again.

Seconds later, he burst through the door. His forehead oozed with sweat. His face glowed bright orange. He shot her an incandescent stare, then turned to his mother.

"They didn't like the presents," he announced.

The driver had overheard. Monisha gulped and sank into her chair. Shailesh ignored her.

She stood up sharply, her head almost clipping the photograph of Mr Kulkarni. "They were joking, Shailesh! It's all fun and games."

Mrs Kulkarni nodded, then rushed off to the kitchen. She returned with a tray of iced lime water. Shailesh took a glass and sipped thoughtfully.

"Then why are you here?"

Monisha tried to remember what Aunt Romila had told her to say, but her heart was pounding too fast. She could pretend she was just passing. But brides wouldn't generally cross town to make visits the day before a wedding. Or would they? She took a deep breath, and tried to explain that the purple-and-green sari didn't suit her. But when she saw Shailesh frowning the words came out jumbled.

At that instant, Ayesha burst into tears and stormed out of the room. Seema toddled off alongside her and Mrs Kulkarni trailed behind them.

"Those colours," said Shailesh through gritted teeth, "were my father's... for his football team."

Suddenly, Monisha felt a sense of Mr Kulkarni's presence. His ice-cold stare on her shoulders. The strong, proud, family man. Snatched away from them, all too early. A chill ran down her spine. She gasped.

"Oh Shailesh! If only I had known..."

"And the saris were like sacks, I hear." He shook his

head and began walking towards his room. Monisha leapt out of her seat and followed him.

His bedroom was dark and sparse. A flimsy watercolour sketch of the elephant god Ganesha hung on the wall. A thin mattress covered in blue-and-white-checked sheets rested on a mahogany bed frame. His wedding outfit drooped on the clothes rail opposite. Its turban dangled from the door. Monisha pulled out the only chair in the room and sat. Miserable and heavy hearted.

But she kept an eye out. At any moment her mother-in-law could walk in. Or Ayesha might bring over an armful of ironed shirts. Such was the privacy! And in two days' time she was supposed to be sleeping here. With *this* man. If he ever forgave her.

Shailesh heaved the door shut. The silk turban swung from side to side. "You girls and your stupid weddings," he hissed. "My sister had to leave her baby and buy all this nonsense for those rich bitches."

It was harsh, but she nodded anyway.

When he saw her, his face swelled with rage. He flung the turban onto the floor and stomped over to his bed. The coins in his pocket clinked and jangled as he collapsed onto the blue-checked sheets.

"If I had it my way, I wouldn't have a stupid, social wedding."

Fear gripped her throat while she watched him, her mouth was parched. Outside the street boys cheered as ball hit bat. She'd have to speak above their shrill cries.

The words came out, just barely. What kind of wedding did he have in mind?

He would have much preferred a registry wedding. And the cash her parents had spent; well, he could have taken it instead.

She picked up the turban from the floor, hung it on the hook and eased back into her chair. Surely he was joking?

"Like… a dowry?"

He shot her an angry glare.

"Of course! I'm a Brahmin surgeon! Why should it cost me to get married when I should be the one getting paid?"

Monisha looked up in horror. This could not be happening. This was not the man she'd sipped shandy with at the Leatherhead Café, in front of its mauve walls and blond hippies. Her stomach churned.

"I thought dowries were illegal."

He told her that dowries were the norm. She shot out of her chair. Her hands began trembling. But she was a doctor! A resident at St Anthony's!

Shailesh marched over to the door and flung the silk turban off the hook, again. It slid across the floor and brushed her leg.

"Do you think you're the only lady doctor looking for a husband? I could have chosen anyone I wanted!"

Monisha covered her ears and started running. The pounding began again in her head, her chest. Her bare feet slapped against the cement floor. She rummaged through the reception room for her sandals. Where the hell were they?

Mrs Kulkarni held them up in front of her face, chewing betel nut as she spoke. Her lips blood red, her teeth brown and jagged.

"Are you looking for these?"

Their silver hearts flashed. Monisha nodded.

"Men say terrible things when they are angry. Then they forget."

Monisha shook her head. There was no way she was going to forgive and forget.

Drool bubbled in the old woman's mouth. She ambled towards the front door, chewing. "Please remember, we were rich once, like yourselves, but we lost everything."

Monisha snatched back her sandals and edged closer to the exit.

"My father is a lecturer and my mother has never worked. That doesn't make us rich."

The old woman spat out a glob of reddish-brown, speckled gunge. Out it flew in a perfect arc, until it landed in a spittoon by the door. An entire mouthful of stinking, saliva-filled betel nut almost filled the earthenware pot.

Monisha turned her face away and shuddered. How disgusting! She had to get out. Out of the flat. Out of the marriage. Right now.

But Mrs Kulkarni and Shailesh were both standing in the doorway.

"What have you said to upset this poor girl, Shailesh?"

He lowered his head until it almost touched his chest, but didn't answer. Mrs Kulkarni sighed and pulled out two chairs. She made them sit, facing each other.

"Shailesh say 'sorry'... And, young lady, you can't just leave like that. We're family."

Monisha groaned.

"Yes, I can."

But there was no arguing now. They had exchanged rings in front of Lord Krishna. And, according to Mrs Kulkarni, that was that.

Shailesh apologised for using the word 'dowry'. What he needed was a loan. Of around $30,000. He promised to repay it.

But that was extortionate! She didn't have that kind of money.

Apparently, it was nothing when you compared it to the going rate for a top civil servant husband: one million US dollars. One million outright!

Monisha covered her ears and got up. Hot tears trickled down her cheeks.

"I can't go through with this," she cried. "It's all too much. Too much!"

At that moment the doorbell rang and Aunt Romila's driver came charging into the reception room pointing at his watch. In a flash she was on her way back to Sitara Road, glum with despair.

15

Aunt Romila's jeep bounced and clunked through the dust and debris of the back streets. Past bright, ragged saris and bony babies. Before blood splattered brick walls. While Monisha sat silently in the passenger seat, with rage bubbling away inside her head. Ready to spew forth any moment, like fiery lava.

What was Shailesh Kulkarni playing at?

He'd been so different the week they'd met: silky haired, suit clad, cool and successful. How had he turned into this money-grabbing monster? Damn that Ayesha! Stupid, reckless girl. She was to blame. Or was she?

He was totally inconsistent. On the one hand, against tradition. He hated bridegroom interviews, bogus astrologers and even wedding receptions. He'd been happy to marry a career woman: a medic from the States.

Even happier to take a dowry.

But what about her aunts and cousins? Poking fun like that. Bitches indeed! Could they have pushed him over the edge?

The sign for Sitara Road flashed before her eyes, and then the gleaming white house. The place she treasured. Outside the marquee was ready now, painstakingly decorated with pale-pink roses and swirls of soft, white tulle. Her mother's choice. She began to sob. Loudly. The driver handed her a handkerchief. He'd blab, but she didn't care. Every inch of her body was now filled with despair. Choky, sickly, achy, vomity despair.

How would her parents take this?

She scrambled out and kept her eyes on the ground. Away from the beautiful marquee. How much could it have cost them? Thousands probably. She'd pay it back in full. Sell her car. Get a loan. The money would be in their account in five working days. Just like in the commercial. And she'd have to cut back on her already spartan lifestyle.

After three half-hearted knocks on the front door she was in. The swirly marble floor sparkled in the mid-afternoon sun. Flies buzzed round the mahogany dining table, which was now hidden under baskets of fruits and flowers. At one end of the sofa sat her father, twiddling his thumbs. Next to him, her mother, eyeing the door.

And, in front of them, stood Shailesh!

Shailesh Kulkarni, her soon to be ex-fiancé with his head bowed low and his motorbike helmet tucked underneath one arm. Sickness whirled through her stomach. Into her throat. *Breathe*, she told herself. Oh dear God, just breathe!

Then everything went dark and tingly.

"Ice, ice," cried Mrs Bastikar.

First, she felt something cold and jagged scraping her cheek. Then, a bangle brushed against her wrist. She opened her eyes and caught sight of her mother kneeling beside her. A scarlet-faced Shailesh hovered over them both. She sat up sharp as a tack.

"I'm sorry, Monisha," he said, before launching into a lengthy explanation about the events of the past few months. He just hadn't been himself. Everything had happened at once: his sister just landed up, then her baby came. The baby needed an operation and…

"I would have liked to have bought you far more, but…"

Leela Bastikar shot up off the floor and immediately sent all the helpers out to the garden. Only when the door was shut behind them did she begin speaking again.

"The gifts were absolutely fine, Shailesh. Monisha, what have you been saying?"

Realising that he might have sparked a row, Shailesh turned his attention towards Professor Bastikar. He sat himself down by his prospective father-in-law's feet, placed his motorbike helmet beside him and began speaking about Ayesha. And how she'd started off as her father's favourite and ended up being gang raped by criminals after his death.

"She's been unlucky too, with poor Seema needing surgery. It almost bankrupted me. That's why I asked Monisha for a loan."

Mrs Bastikar gasped. Professor Bastikar's eyebrows curled together into a knot. Shailesh fidgeted in front of them, tapping the shiny surface of his helmet.

"But you said you should have been paid a dowry," protested Monisha, "and you asked for $30,000!"

Leela Bastikar shrieked so loudly that it triggered a coughing fit. Monisha called for water, but the helpers were all outside, so she ran off to get some. Shailesh tried speaking above them. He hadn't meant to use the d-word. It was just a loan he needed. Honestly!

Professor Bastikar looked at him gravely. The young man in front of him was clearly suffering from familiar afflictions: a 'cash crisis' and 'family trouble'. Both could be eradicated with a one-way ticket to the States. Once upon a time, he'd used the same remedy.

"You have been through a very difficult time, Shailesh," he said. "Things will get better."

Monisha's emotions began to run haywire. Suddenly she felt a surge of compassion. Poor Shailesh! Just when he was trying to establish himself, his sister's divorce and Seema's operation had hit him out of nowhere. He had only done the decent thing by helping them. And got into debt. But $30,000 was still too much.

Her father delivered welcome news: there would be cash gifts at the wedding. And, of course, when he moved to the States, the dollars would start coming in.

Shailesh nodded like an obedient schoolboy.

Leela Bastikar stared nervously at the clock, then at her son-in-law.

"Now that we have reached a solution, Shailesh, I must ask you to leave. It's bad luck for the bride and groom to see each other after dusk."

"What poppycock!" exclaimed Professor Bastikar.

"You stick to $E = mc^2$, Amit!" retorted his wife.

And, after what seemed like an eternity, the joyous sound of laughter filled the air. Leela Bastikar ushered Shailesh towards the front door. Monisha watched him from her window until he disappeared into the pitch-black night.

16

It was half past seven in the morning. The smog filled air above Sitara Road was thick with tension and excitement. The wedding marquee now drooped under the weight of its floral decorations. Scents of sandalwood incense and burning butter wafted throughout the house. In the kitchen, Aunt Romila shouted orders over the hissing and spluttering of hot oil, while Leela Bastikar scurried back and forth, checking on everything.

Upstairs, the makeup lady traced around Monisha's eyes with kohl, and hooked the golden tikka onto her parting. And suddenly it happened. The transformation she'd been waiting for all her life. A beautiful bride beamed back in the mirror. Bedecked in jewels from head to toe, and wrapped in luxurious, green-and-gold silk. Just like in the movies. Except that her nose throbbed from the tug of its ring and chain. And the petticoat was so tight she could barely breathe.

She staggered to the window for fresh air. The groom's party were already here! Outside they marched, with Shailesh at the front, in his cream silk robes. Seema skipping along next to him in pink. Aunties, uncles and cousins, in rows of four.

And Ayesha, pale and beautiful, in apricot chiffon.

A chill ran through her spine. Then the thorns began to prick. If it hadn't been for Ayesha there would be no debt. Prick. Shailesh would never have mentioned the d-word. Prick. And this day would have been a truly happy one. Prick.

The sound of her mother's footsteps caught her by surprise.

"Where's Mrs Kulkarni?" There was no way she could bring herself to call the old woman anything else.

Her mother told her that widows were barred from auspicious occasions.

"But why?"

Mrs Bastikar slapped a wad of cash onto the makeup lady's palm and sent the woman on her way.

"Widows are bad omens, Monisha – a reminder of sorrow and loss."

But what about the old lady's sorrow and loss? Were widowers banned as well? There were so many traditions in Indian weddings that didn't make sense to her, like dowries for instance. How long had they been around? And why were they still around when women were earning?

According to her mother, it was the Europeans who'd started the tradition. But somehow they'd managed to relieve themselves of it and dump it on India.

Other little questions burned inside.

"Why hadn't Shailesh just taken a bank loan?"

Aunt Romila knocked on the door. Downstairs a crowd had gathered.

"Indian men grow up knowing they'll get money through marriage," whispered Mrs Bastikar.

Monisha grimaced. Was this how it was meant to be? The best day in her life? Beginning with a $30,000 debt and an emotional roller coaster ride. With Shailesh assuming he'd be paid to marry her. She froze.

The knocks became louder, more frantic. The priest could not be kept waiting. For wedding rituals, timings were sacrosanct.

Leela Bastikar stared at herself in the mirror, and adjusted the folds of her sari until each one was stiff and perfect. Then she strutted over to her daughter and gently lifted up her wedding veil.

"My dear girl, don't ruin your beautiful face with that look."

Now Monisha had no choice. She took in a deep breath and smiled the smile that all Indian brides spent years rehearsing.

The next seven hours went like a dream. First the prayers to welcome the groom and the blessings for the couple. Afterwards, a white cloth was placed between herself and Shailesh as the priest recited the story of Tapati, the daughter of the sun-god and her marriage to a virtuous king.

Up, up, up went the cloth when he'd finished. And, for the first time, Shailesh looked into her eyes. Not his usual two second glance. But fully. Deeply. So deeply that the dowry and debt were forgotten for a moment. Her heart skipped a beat.

Then, down came the rice and confetti. Frosting up in piles. And, everywhere, the smell of incense. Flickering flames, flashes of gold and silver. So intoxicating! She was high. Really high! High, like the drug addicts who hung round Highgate Mall.

Her jasmine garland felt as light as a feather. Over his neck, she placed his, standing on tiptoes. A cocky smile lit her lips. He was tall, thank God!

Then the most famous part of all. Round the holy fire, seven times. One for sap. Two for juice. Seven times for seven lives. She knew it off by heart. Her hand across his chest as he spoke the words.

"Dear wife, by taking these seven steps, you have become my dearest friend."

A thrill soared up through her ankles.

"Go again," shouted the crowd. "That was only six."

"Okay then, just to be sure," yelled Aunt Romila.

And round they went once more.

At last, he applied the powder on her parting. In a perfectly straight line. Like a surgeon's cut, they cried. Thick red dust whooshed into the air. Some landed on her nose. A sign of good luck.

Her turn now. Oh God. Oh God. The sandalwood paste for his forehead was a slushy mess.

"It's a zigzag," screeched Riya. "You've started a new trend!"

More laughter. Then rice and confetti. Hoots. Cheers. Ear-piercing whistles. Everything warm and fuzzy, her head starting to spin.

It was over. They were married. Eleven months after they'd met. Four days after she'd landed in Mumbai. And one night after a heated argument.

That evening, the Taj Mahal Palace Hotel buzzed with guests. Scribbled on a chalkboard outside the conference room were the words: 'Dr Shailesh Kulkarni, Mrs Monisha Kulkarni and wedding party'.

It took a while for it to sink in.

For the next two hours, Shailesh and Monisha stood in the doorway, flashing painted on smiles for guests and gatecrashers. When they were done, silver trays of sizzling kebabs awaited them. Naan and tandoori breads were puffed up like pillows.

Everything was perfect. Just as she'd always wanted it.

After the party ended, the couple made their way into the bridal suite. When the lights came on, she saw the king-sized bed blanketed by rose petals. Shailesh pulled her close. Time stood still as he struggled with her hooks, chains and pins. Suddenly her hairpiece rolled off her head and onto the floor.

"My, what thick tresses of hair you have!" he joked.

Together they burst out laughing.

She glanced over at the mirror, the kohl was still thick round her eyes and her lips dusty-pink. He took her henna-stained hand and lay down on the bed. Thump! Thump! Her heart raced faster and faster. Tina's words came catapulting back.

"Try to get drunk, the first time will really hurt."

She peeked round the room. No alcohol. None whatsoever.

He leant over to kiss her. Betel nut and onions on his breath. Ugh! She pulled away and buried her face in the petals on her pillow.

"What's wrong?"

After a brief silence, she closed her eyes, held her breath and relented. His belly rolled over her, flattening her like dough. Then he charged into her like a crazed bull. Tearing her insides to shreds. She prayed for the torture to end.

"Oh, dear Lord!" she screamed when it was over.

Soon the royal bridal room reverberated with his deafening snores. Her mind flashed back to the wintry evening in Café Uno. And Tina's interrogation.

"Don't you want to know what he's like in bed?"

Well, now she knew.

17

The Kulkarni's flat looked more shabby than chic. Golden paper chains and jasmine garlands had been slung on just about anything, from photographs to furniture. Sticks of incense lined the hallway. Red vermillion symbols were splashed across the walls. The landlords had been very understanding; it was, after all, for a wedding.

Monisha's foot tipped over the clay pot filled with rice, scattering grains across the reception room; the new bride would bring abundance and prosperity. Shailesh clop-clopped along beside her, in ugly, buckled sandals, his shawl knotted tightly into her sari. Cameras clicked in their faces while Mrs Kulkarni plied them with sickly sweets.

It was all beginning to drive her crazy.

After a sore and sleepless night, she'd been shaken out of bed by the makeup lady's relentless knocking. For the lunch reception, her 'look' had to complement the purple-

and-green 'football team' sari. All morning, her hair was pulled and crimped, and every shade of lipstick and rouge tested in hope.

By the time Monisha had made it down to eat, the biryani was ice cold. In the most humiliating fashion, she'd started choking on a cube of lamb and had to be Heimliched by Saurav Das, in front of the wedding guests. How would she ever live that down?

When the drama was over, she was packed into the bridal car and dispatched to Sitara Road for the official farewell. There she'd walked through the courtyard, throwing fistfuls of rice over her shoulder, while her mother and father sobbed. Each foot had felt like lead; the sound of their tears had ripped her heart in two.

"Don't look back, Monisha," Aunt Romila had said. "You are part of the Kulkarni family now."

Ouch! That stung. Was it so simple? Some prayers in front of a fire, a judge's signature and you defected to the other side?

"I'm still Monisha Bastikar," she'd protested before Shailesh shot her a fearsome glare. He'd wanted her to change her name to 'Kulkarni', but she'd made excuses. Everything she'd achieved so far, was as a Bastikar. From her driving licence to her medical licence. She couldn't possibly change it now.

As the crowd of guests slowly dispersed, Monisha stumbled in to Shailesh's bedroom, dizzy from the smell of incense. Everything in it was brand new, the bed, the dresser and the pine wardrobes. She rubbed her hands against the glossy wood. All of it was gifted by her parents, and so much more tasteful and elegant than what was there before.

Shailesh ignored her show of approval and announced that he was taking his mother to the temple. Monisha felt like a caged bird being set free. As the front door banged shut, she curled up on the bridal bed, pulled the dazzling red-gold blanket over herself and shut her eyes.

The sound of Ayesha's voice made her jump.

"I can't wait until Shailesh lives with you in America."

Monisha closed her eyes again and turned over.

"Things will be so different when I marry Chemjong."

Chemjong? Had she heard that correctly? What an exotic sounding name! Surely her sister-in-law wasn't getting married. She wasn't even divorced! Now Monisha couldn't sleep, even if she wanted to. She had to ask. Who on earth was Chemjong?

Ayesha picked up a cloth and began dusting the window ledges. Just as she'd finished one, the road dirt stealthily crept back in. Chemjong was a Nepalese Christian. His family owned a tailoring business. And, as to be expected, her mother didn't approve of him.

For a second, her sister-in-law's usually expressionless face lit up. But soon she swung her head back round, leaving only her rope-like plait in view.

Ayesha dropped her cloth and spoke to the street.

"I haven't told Shailesh anything. He won't be happy."

She began dusting again, vigorously. Her mother had apparently told her to forget Chemjong and take up yoga instead. Monisha stared at her blankly.

"You know… the exercises that… block your desires." Ayesha began giggling, though it wasn't remotely funny.

"Anyway, she'll be living with you, in America."

There it was, the bitter truth. Her aunts had warned her. The only son. Completely expected of him. Monisha began to feel queasy. Mrs Kulkarni with her seven cloves of garlic, in the tiny Northend flat. Spewing betel nut everywhere.

"But what about you and Seema?"

Ayesha stared dreamily out the window. Apparently Chemjong loved Seema. And she loved him. They were almost a family.

It was late evening when Shailesh returned with his mother, leaving time for only a quiet supper in the flat. Mrs Kulkarni had prepared something simple. Soft, warm chapattis and mixed vegetable curry.

"After all that heavy wedding food."

Monisha ate in silence. Not long now and they'd be on the train to Goa. Just the two of them, in the first-class, air-conditioned carriage. On a well-deserved holiday, with no in-laws butting their noses in.

"Ayesha will pack your suitcase," said Mrs Kulkarni. "She's an expert."

The old lady had hijacked her thoughts. She was determined to destroy them.

Monisha shook her head and headed towards her bedroom. She'd rather do it herself, she told her. Ayesha slithered in behind her.

"Why don't you let her pack it?" called Shailesh. "She knows my stuff. I'll never find it otherwise."

Ayesha beamed from ear to ear.

"No!" cried Monisha, before lowering her voice. "I mean, Ayesha is busy enough. And if you packed your own things Shailesh, you'd find them."

Suddenly, a deathly silence descended upon the flat. The smile rapidly disappeared from Ayesha's face. Mrs Kulkarni glowered, and a red-hot frown flickered across her forehead. Shailesh looked perplexed.

There they stood in the doorway, ganged up like in a Bollywood film. The scowling mother-in-law, her feckless son and the divorcee daughter with a double life.

Monisha turned her back to them as gently as she could and began arranging her underwear into neat little bundles. When she picked up the racy, red silk chemise chosen by Riya, the Kulkarnis scattered sharply.

It was another hour before the taxi arrived. Monisha almost tripped over herself in her rush to get away.

18

As the doors to the Juliet balcony flew open, Anjuna Beach shimmered into view. Miles of turquoise water and white sand. Here, there were only gentle sounds: The tide rolling in. A child's laughter. Seagulls. No deafening car horns or trumpeting rickshaws.

Goa was magical, healing. Just what she needed.

Every morning, Monisha sauntered along the terrace to catch some sun. Ooh, its tingling warmth! Darker skin wasn't a problem now that she was married.

Flouncing around in flared skirts, beside her husband, she discovered the bliss of couple-dom. Strolling on the beach hand in hand. Nibbling on fried corn and pakoras. Curling up in bed to watch Bollywood films. And the ultimate luxury, a jacuzzi.

But, after a few days of their cosy routine, a nagging question burned inside. When were they ever going to start their life together?

Shailesh had spoken about all the patients waiting for operations when he got back and finding a good nursery for Seema. He was looking into courses for Ayesha, to help her with her sewing business. He hadn't mentioned coming to the States once.

Rage simmered away inside her, but Monisha kept it hidden. When he rambled on about his family, she feigned interest, nodded and agreed. Even though she knew Ayesha wanted nothing more than to marry Chemjong and sew in his shop. And that Seema wouldn't need a nursery until she was three. Why should she upset the apple cart? She would only ruin blissful memories. Spoil the tranquillity around her.

By the fifth day, she was ready to explode. When she found Shailesh laying on a sun lounger, with his nose buried deep in the latest Wilbur Smith, she fired off. Like a cannonball.

"So, when *do* you start in Wichita?"

"Whenever I want," replied Shailesh with his head firmly in the book.

Monisha removed her sunglasses so he could see her frown. But he took no notice and continued reading. Her voice rose to a shrill pitch, like her mother's did, in front of a disobedient Swanker.

"What kind of job has no start date?"

He told her it was an observership. Monisha cringed.

"What's the stipend?"

Suddenly, Shailesh banged his book shut and looked up at her.

"There is none."

A child's ice cream tumbled onto the sand. First came loud, whiny tears, then the screeching of gulls. All fell silent when one swooped down and snatched it. Monisha shook out a towel and flung it over the sunlounger beside Shailesh. After giving him the frostiest of stares, she plonked herself down. The wood rattled under her thighs. Awkwardly.

"Why have you taken a job that won't pay?"

It was a foot in the door, he told her, to make contacts and to get a local referee. But it was all very confusing. Wasn't Professor Sawhney his local referee?

Shailesh sat up, tucked his book under his arm and eased his feet into his sandals.

"He's never seen me work," he said shrugging his shoulders. "I'm going to get ice cream."

His face glistened red and black with sweat. Wet stubble sprouted along his chin. A mound of fat had collected on his belly and etched below were the elastic markings from his shorts. This was not the smooth, sophisticated Shailesh from their first meeting. This was Shailesh, the fattened-up, oily-haired liar. Fumbling his explanations, dancing round the truth. About to scarper.

He got up and began walking. Quicker and quicker. Monisha shot off behind him. Bare feet burning on hot sand.

"So, you expect *me* to support you? "

"Nonsense! Why do you think I want to stay back?"

He said it would be for a few months. A year. To get the rent in order. Once Ayesha started up her business properly, they'd be fine.

A year.

The fluttering began again. Another twelve months in Northend. Alone. Oh God! Unless you counted Miss

Never There and Mr Don't Wake Me. Sundays wasted, traipsing round: ghost–like. Through the Mall. Into the Laundromat. Onto the tin stool. Waiting for the last spin. Waiting for her husband.

Oh God! Her mother's ghastly newsflashes: *'Verma daughter-in-law expecting. Ravi Sinha has a brand-new house. Essex Junction. Six bedrooms. Nanny-room as well. With en suite!'*

Shailesh held out an ice cream and waved it in front of her. She folded her arms tightly and shook her head. He insisted. The vendor was getting irate. A queue had formed.

She took it. Licked it with reluctance. It was sickly strawberry, like cough syrup. Ugh! Being made to down this, along with everything else.

But why was Shailesh abandoning his wife to stay with his family, when they didn't need him anymore?

"What's that supposed to mean?" he growled when he heard the question.

Monisha edged closer towards him. Her hands, flat and upright. "It means, we should be thinking about *us*. Not Ayesha. She has her own life now… and she won't be needing any courses!"

Then it all spilled out, like a giant tidal wave. Ayesha dreamy eyed, dusting. Secretly in love with Chemjong, the Nepalese Christian with a tailoring business. Sewing together. Raising Seema. Mrs Kulkarni telling her daughter to do yoga. How ridiculous!

"Not as ridiculous as what I've just heard," said Shailesh. His voice rose to a thundering boom. "That girl is going to finish me off completely!"

He tossed his half-eaten ice cream into the bin. Monisha followed suit. Heart pounding loudly. Poor Ayesha. Had her sister in-law told her about Chemjong in confidence? Or because she *wanted* her brother to find out?

And whose side was she supposed to be on now? She took a deep breath, like when facing Professor Folstein. She told him that it was all good news. Ayesha had found someone decent to support her and help raise her child. Someone financially secure. But Shailesh grabbed his towel and began walking towards the hotel.

Back turned he shouted.

"How do you know he's decent? And what about Seema? Running around a tailoring shop, and being raised by a bunch of…" He checked that there were no Goans within earshot. "Christians!"

"But Shailesh…"

He continued walking. Ignoring her. Like she was a beggar child. A hanger-on. She sprinted up beside him and grabbed his arm.

"Ayesha is responsible for her daughter! You have your own marriage to think about. And residency jobs…"

"You Americans are so naïve. You think everything works the same way here as it does *over there!*"

Over here. Over there. Her argument with Tina.

Tears began rolling down her cheeks.

"I just want us to be happy, Shailesh… and Ayesha."

Brief, muffled sobs trickled through. Wasn't that what he wanted too?

That evening a chilly wind blew hard along Anjuna Beach. Specks of sand spun through the air then into eyes and faces. The hotel's pretty mosaic floors turned ice cold. And in the honeymoon suite there was complete silence. Broken only by the jarring buzz of the room-service bell.

19

New England winters were bleak. The sun peeped in at seven and was gone by half past three. You'd leave home and come home in pitch black. That was on good days. It was the bad days that Monisha dreaded, when the street lay buried under a blanket of snow. Anyone else could ring in with excuses – *"School's shut! Timmy and Maisie can't be left!"* – then spend the day sledging. It was the child-free who had to stay in work.

That meant huddling in with other miserable medics, and buying overpriced deodorant and toothpaste from the shop on the ground floor. Or lining up for leftovers in the canteen. Only storeroom staples now. Bean stew. Tuna and beans. Tomato and bean soup. She hated winter. Hated it. Hated it. Hated it!

And when she thought of Shailesh scoffing samosas in sunny Mumbai, she hated him too. Almost a year and *still* he hadn't come.

Only the wedding video reminded her they were married, and it had been ruthlessly edited. Everything so picture perfect. None of the haughty laughter as she opened up his meagre gifts. Nor the shock on her face. Just the twanging of sitars then a still of her henna-lined hands!

And everyone dazzled in gold and silk splendour. Women fluttered their kohl-lined lids. Children raced round in oversized kurtas. Her own mother and father grinned from ear to ear, blessing their beloved son-in-law. *And to think twelve hours before he'd begged for a dowry!*

Long wintry nights passed by. Outside the wind and rain whooshed and spluttered. Alone in her single bed, Monisha would ask herself if it had it all really happened. In an instant, she'd leap out and switch on the video. Just to be sure.

She would fast forward it, freeze it. Yes, they had walked round the holy fire seven times. And there it was! That mucky sandalwood zigzag, running down his forehead. Shailesh was *definitely* her husband now.

The minute it hit, she'd flick to *Saturday Night Live*, tight throated, hoping that a comic routine would make her laugh. It didn't. It couldn't.

Her 'marriage' consisted of a couple of emails each week. Mainly Kulkarni trumpet blowing. Full operating lists in summertime. Seema heading for the best nursery in the state. Ayesha now the most magnificent seamstress in Mumbai. Of course, Chemjong never got a mention.

Then that gushing apology. Shailesh couldn't make it over in the fall. His mother was laid up in bed with her bad back. Oh yes! The bad back that never bothered her when she stood for hours making his favourite curry or when she lifted his giant baskets of washing.

He had asked Monisha to take a trip to Mumbai. But squeeze herself into that tiny flat with the Kulkarni women? And watch them fetch and carry for him all day? No thank you! She made her excuses and fled to New York with Tina for as long as her wallet permitted: five glorious days.

They did Central Park, took in its spectacular spruces and elegant elms. Tina jogging, with red curls fluttering. Monisha walking as fast as she could. Anxiously anticipating another interrogation.

Tina bouncing. Knees, shoulders, calves and curls in rhythm. Even her words kept time.

"There's no point asking you about your marriage. It hasn't started yet."

Monisha thought she'd been let off the hook, but Tina hadn't finished. She'd ranted loudly. In front of other joggers, who weren't wearing headphones.

"And that woman in your wedding video wasn't you! It was a body double, wearing a nose ring and a wig, like one of those hideous queens in the *Kama Sutra*!"

A ripple of laughter had followed, and that stung. So hard in fact, that she'd had to bend down and take a breath. So hard, that Tina paid for dinner that night. And they'd racked up quite a bill at Angelo's. Fortunately, free fettuccine alfredo worked wonders, so the friendship continued.

It was almost springtime before Shailesh came over. And when Monisha saw him wandering through Logan International, bedraggled, with more belly fat and less hair than last time, she felt nothing. Not love. Not joy. Not even relief.

Just nothing.

He smiled at her. But only a half-smile. Like he'd left the other half in Mumbai.

The exit from the airport was confusing. Twirling loops of freeway sprouted everywhere. One wrong turn and they'd be lost. Monisha hunched over in the driver's seat, searching desperately for the 'North' sign.

Shailesh called her a safe but boring driver, and suggested they stop for a drink. A traffic light appeared out of nowhere. She slammed the brakes.

"This is the US; you can't drink and drive."

"Okay. I'll drink, you drive."

The streets were busy. There were 'Sale' signs plastered on every window. A woman with a baby stroller crossed the street. Inside, Monisha's anger burned hot. Here, she was the breadwinner. And he owed her. He drink and she drive? Grr! Just like Sohan Singh had thought. And what had her mother said?

"I'm not your taxi. Goddam it!"

A shocked silence followed. Less than an hour out of customs and an argument was brewing. Shailesh spoke in a soft, barely audible muffle.

"After I've dumped my things, maybe we could go out later and both of us grab something to eat and… er, drink."

She chuckled to herself. With those exam scores, he was obviously a brilliant student. And he was learning already.

They reached Northend. Monisha nervously unlocked the door to the flat. In the lounge, the small TV was on.

Blonde presenters with fake tans lit up the room. Mr Anaesthesiology was sitting on the sofa, rather close to another man. Shailesh dragged his dusty suitcases in. She winced. They smelled of diesel and drainpipes.

"My husband, Shailesh," she announced. "He'll be staying a few days."

It sounded almost apologetic. Mr Anaesthesiology looked up and nodded a hello. The man next to him pouted.

"My boyfriend, Jack. We were just leaving."

Shailesh grimaced and let out an audible groan. The two thin men walked straight into the smell of diesel and drainpipes, before slipping out the door. Monisha felt herself blush.

"HOMOSEXUALS!" shouted Shailesh, eyes ablaze. "I can't stay here!"

Monisha rushed over to the kitchen in search of a cloth and disinfectant. She didn't know anything about her flat mate, except that he was an anaesthesiologist. The rest was irrelevant, she told Shailesh before complaining that his suitcases stank. He raised his eyebrows.

"But you have homosexuals in your flat!"

Monisha wiped the baggage. Over and over, until a sickly smell of pine needles prevailed.

Shailesh waved his arms in the air. "I can't stay here, with those two... in bed together. Bleurgh!"

"Well, I can't afford a hotel."

She placed a large towel on the floor of Miss Never There's room and dragged one of the suitcases in. Shailesh followed with the other. There was now barely space to stand.

When they finally got to her own room, Shailesh rang his mother. His voice choked as he spoke. Tears welled up in his eyes. Yes, he'd reached safely. Yes, America was really clean. The streets were wide. The buildings were grey.

When Seema came on, he began sobbing. Monisha gently placed a hand on his shoulder. It was a while before he could compose himself.

"Ayesha wants to talk with you."

Goodness knew why! Monisha took the receiver hesitantly. A moment later, she was all smiles.

"She's married Chemjong! The pictures are on the internet. They're about to leave for their honeymoon."

Shailesh frowned deeply. "Stupid, stupid girl."

He watched helplessly as each image came through. The bride in a cream silk sari. Chemjong, smart in his crisp, black suit. Seema their flower girl. And Mrs Kulkarni beaming. All perfectly timed, to take place the minute her brother left for the States. Clever move, Ayesha. The sly fox.

That night, at the Cheers Bar, Shailesh sulked in front of his Jack Daniels. Monisha picked up a bar bill of $150.

Their married life together had officially begun.

20

The days whirled ahead and vanished one by one, into a pool of lost time. A few weeks passed before they could see each other. There was always some obstacle that prevented them. Shailesh hadn't found the right apartment yet. Monisha was asked to cover for a colleague. Someone dropped out of a laparoscopy workshop and suddenly Shailesh had a free place. Then came the problem of aeroplane tickets, expensive and available, or cheap and not. Co-ordinating their diaries made her head spin.

The journey over to Wichita was just as she'd expected. Tedious. After a delayed connection and four packets of potato crisps, Monisha reached the airport. Moments later Shailesh came charging into the meeting point, so quickly that he nearly knocked her over.

He appeared rested and carefree, as if he were on holiday. His belly was now hidden beneath his handknitted jumper, one of Mrs Kulkarni's creations. He chatted away excitedly about his new car, an absolute bargain. He'd had to buy one. Hutchinson was forty miles out and there was no other way to get around town.

The old bomber was fire-engine red. When it started making spluttering noises, Monisha burst out laughing. It let out a deafening 'VROOM VROOM' and she began quivering.

Shailesh leant over her and reached into the glove box and lifted out a gift-wrapped package. She felt it; it was hard, flat and rectangular.

"What do you think of this?"

Perplexed, she opened the gift. It was a solitary wall tile. Blue with a hand-painted sunflower.

"The first piece of our first house."

She threw her arms round him. He kissed her, tenderly. A thrill soared through her body. Her hairs stood on end.

Oh my God! This was really happening!

The Three Oaks apartment block was more like a holiday villa; a white facade, yellow shuttered windows and a sandstone courtyard that led to the pool. Shailesh's flat was on the ground floor. She couldn't help but feel jealous; all of it came for less than half of what she was paying for her room at Northend.

The front door was flung open. Cayenne pepper and curry spices hit her nostrils and made her cough. A young man rushed over to greet her: five foot two, Indian, with hands yellowed by turmeric and the filthiest of fingernails. She gagged and gasped.

"Pleased to meet you, Monisha. I'm Suresh," he said. "Your cook for today."

Trying hard not to think about his fingernails, she turned her attention towards the living room, which was jam-packed with odd bits of furniture: a black leather couch with torn cushions, and a pine table and four cane chairs. Books with an array of titles were stacked high on the floor: *Engineering Basics*, *Windows for Dummies* and *Gallbladder Surgery*. And the carpet had been destroyed by shoe marks.

A blast of Bollywood music made her jump. Another man appeared, his white polo shirt gleaming against jet-black skin. He swaggered over, clapping his hands in time with the beat.

"I'm Rajan. What'll it be, Shailesh?"

He searched for an unused whisky glass in vain.

"A top up, Suresh?"

No drink offered to her. Not even lemonade.

Shailesh nodded, then took her bag and dumped it in a room that smelled of pickles. Their flat mate was out of town. His mother had sent him three giant jars.

"You can use this until he's back." said Shailesh.

She raised her eyebrows.

"My room's the smallest."

It was indeed. But, somehow, he'd managed to fit an assortment of single malt whiskies, rum, vodka and wines onto his bedside table. And a stack of beers in a cooler, beneath the dresser.

Monisha clasped her head in her hands. Oily pickles, unemptied trash cans and dirty fingernails. Filth! Filth! Filth! Aargh! She was trapped in a jungle of maleness. And the only way out of it was to cook and clean.

Before he could pick up his whisky glass, she begged Shailesh to drive her to the nearest store.

Three hours later each room had been wiped down and vacuumed. At the dining table, plates and glassware glistened. And they all sat down to supper: chicken curry, fried rice and salad. The men sang her praises and devoured the lot.

Afterwards they sank onto the torn leather couch, drinks in hand, to watch the cricket. Quietly, she slipped out.

The kitchen was a safe haven, away from the drunken discussion on who was the better captain or the best bowler. She started on the dishes. Watching specks of curry disappear into lemony foam seemed far more interesting.

A few minutes later, Shailesh poked his head in.

"Rajan's brother has a degree in physics. I told him your father would get him a job."

He was slurring his words. Monisha glared briefly, but went on washing, stacking the plates onto their holder, then wiping the work surfaces, and restoring cleanliness and order.

She was summoned again. Suresh had thrown up on the carpet. No apology. Only an explanation. Two-day-old red wine and Captain Creole rum, one after another. Nothing to do with her cooking.

Asshole!

Several hours after a tedious two-plane journey, she was cleaning a shoe-and-vomit-stained floor. She scrubbed away. Harder and harder. Tears welling up.

Assholes! Assholes! Assholes!

When she was done, she headed to the bathroom. Shailesh followed her.

"I can't believe you told him my father would get his brother a job!"

He was wobbling. His face now as red as his car. His voice thick and heavy, his words garbled.

"This is what Indians do: help each other."

She banged the door in his face.

"AND WASTE THEIR MONEY ON DRINK... WHICH THEY CAN'T HANDLE."

Hot water trickled from the shower, then burst through at full speed. Rose and damask infused her senses. Bought from the local store, a different shower gel for each day. The perfect antidote to all the filth.

Monisha made her way over to Shailesh' s room, feeling warm, delicately scented and contrite. After all, the dinner had ended no differently to others. Drunken men boasting. Women cleaning. She opened her mouth to apologise, but Shailesh was fast asleep. He lay, curled up in front of his drinks cabinet; his quilt in the shape of a large hill.

Luckily, the room that smelled of pickles had a computer. Even better, its username and password were taped to the screen. As Monisha typed away, the machine came to life. Her inbox flashed. A message from Tina.

She was returning to Vermont, she'd found a law firm and a nice apartment. Tina was coming home! Her heart raced. Yippee!

Less enthusiastically, she opened the attachment from Ayesha. It was a picture of herself and Chemjong, with his hand across her belly. The caption in bold letters read 'Number two on the way'.

Monisha shot out of her chair and kicked the floor. A row of stinking running shoes went flying across the room. She bent down to pick them up, trying to hold her breath as the tears flowed. Lord Venkateshwara stared blankly from his resting place, while Shailesh's deafening snores reverberated down the corridor. She sighed and opened the window.

Right now, all she could do was try to get some sleep.

21

The Belvedere Hotel was buzzing with Indian people. Huddled under the brass chandeliers were the latest arrivals, the IT crowd, couples mainly, with one or no kids. And Leela Bastikar had invited them all to the reception dinner.

In the foyer, Shailesh strutted around introducing himself and making small talk. Monisha hovered tentatively behind, in pink silk. She barely knew a soul here. In fact, she barely even knew her husband. A year and a half after their marriage, they had lived together for four weeks. Shock horror!

One month out of eighteen.

The ballroom had been decked out with butterflies of gold-and-silver papier mâché. There were butterfly napkin holders at the table and butterfly king prawns on the menu. According to Leela Bastikar butterflies were good omens; they made dreams come true.

"We can use all this again, for Swanker's reception," Professor Bastikar had said when he surveyed the expensive scene. "Except for the butterfly king prawns… at $8 a head."

But Mrs Bastikar, hobbling round in toned-down, mother-in-law peach, had spared no expense. Linking arms with Shailesh, she made her way into the ballroom. Her sugar-coated voice, once reserved for bridegrooms, was now used on guests.

"My son-in-law Dr Shailesh Kulkarni. MBBS Karnataka. MS Mumbai. Please see the board for your name and table number."

She repeated herself, adding bits as she went.

"My son-in-law Dr Shailesh Kulkarni. MS Mumbai. Working in the department of surgery at Wichita. My daughter Monisha, medical resident at St Anthony's. Please take your seats."

Monisha blushed and looked down at her feet. What airbrushed facts! Shailesh was an observer at Hutchinson, moonlighting in the billing department. But, to her mother, this was minutiae.

Tina strolled by, wearing a green velvet dress and holding a matching clutch. With her hair braided neatly and very little skin on show, she was obviously drumming up business for the firm. Shailesh reached out to her and planted a kiss on her cheek.

"I've heard about you," he said, his face breaking into a smile.

"Well, I've heard very little about you," she replied. Tina immediately turned towards Monisha and hugged her. "I hope you've put me next to someone with a legal problem!"

The head table was at the front and Mrs Bastikar made sure the Vermas were on it. Vinod Verma was no longer president of the Cultural Association but, with his thriving business, stunning mansion, two ex-Ivy-League children and three grandchildren, to Mrs Bastikar, he still stood at the very top of the leaderboard.

On the table next door, Swanker and his friends hooted and giggled with Tina. Monisha stared wistfully. She was trapped next to old snake eyes. Her mind flashed back to that awful encounter. In this very ballroom! Having to explain that she was still a virgin, staring at his pock-marked skin. She'd almost died.

"To have made it over here is quite an achievement, Shailesh," said Vinod Verma. "After losing your father, looking after your sister… her child…" He began pouring out wine. "Red or white for you?"

Shailesh shook his head and lifted out a bottle of sparkling water from the basket.

"I don't drink in front of my elders and certainly not in front of my father-in-law."

The table shook with laughter. Even Monisha laughed at the irony. He was running a bar in his bedroom.

"Monisha, you have definitely found a good Indian boy," said Vinod Verma. "I'd never have thought."

Saurav Das, the nephrologist immediately screwed up his face.

"Why ever not, Vinod? Such a beautiful, qualified girl?" He threw a glance at Shailesh. "So, what exactly are you doing in the… er… department of surgery?"

Shailesh cobbled together an explanation. He wasn't in the university hospital, but working as an observer at

Hutchinson, assisting mainly and waiting for a placement nearer his wife. He'd done a lot of operating in Mumbai and he'd abandoned his burgeoning practice to come to the States.

Saurav Das sipped his wine slowly, without for a second taking his eyes off Shailesh.

"I hope you realise that getting into a surgical residency in the US is almost as difficult as getting into the Whitehouse."

There was silence. Creepy and unpleasant. It was Swati Das who came to the rescue. "Ah look!" she cried, gently brushing her husband's arm. "The butterfly king prawns! And Amit has made us promise to eat every one of them."

Dr Das accepted his caution. By now, everyone knew that the prawns were $8 a head. Vinod Verma said he could have got them cheaper. Amit Bastikar grimaced. The ladies bit into each delicious prawn, wiping lipstick and breadcrumbs off their mouths. The men filled their glasses again and again.

Monisha beamed away as she watched Shailesh. Smart in navy blue. Swimming and lifting weights now. Waiting for a job nearer her. She thought of his beautiful gift of the wall tile, the first piece of their first house.

Underneath the table, she slipped off her sandal and rubbed her foot along his leg. He held her hand, squeezing it tight.

After dinner, the place erupted with jingly Bollywood tunes and ear bursting Bhangra. Shailesh and Monisha stepped onto the dancefloor gracefully, still holding hands. The IT crowd shuffled along behind them. Saris and kurtas flapped and dazzled under the glittery lights.

Soon enough, aunties and uncles joined in, wiggling their flabby midriffs as best they could, until the music became a mesmerising rave.

When the slow dancing was over, the guests left one by one. Shailesh and Monisha crept up to their room. And for the first time in months they made love. Passionately.

Their Belvedere honeymoon suite and bottle of champagne came courtesy of old snake eyes.

22

Before the summer ended there was another trip to Wichita. With the swimming pool and sun loungers, at Three Oaks, it felt like a real holiday. Finally, Monisha could kick her heels up and relax. Now that they were both earning, she didn't have to slave away in the kitchen. They dined out – Italian, Chinese, even Mexican – and slipped out for gelato late at night. Everywhere was food heaven! Mmm!

In Shailesh's room, his bedside table was filled with exotic spirits. Fancy named liqueurs in exquisite bottles: Cointreau, Frangelico and Laphroaig. And he was lapping them up; his cheeks were fatter, redder.

The drinking was beginning to bother her. Each time she watched him fill his glass, there came a twinge of discontent. But she didn't want to pick an argument. Why spoil her break? He wasn't drinking and driving, or missing work. *Or was he?*

The worst part was the snoring. It was a complete nuisance. The only way she could sleep next to him was to have a drink herself. A tot of whisky would put her out like a light.

When she got back to Boston, she noticed she was late. One missed period hadn't caused alarm. Stress. Travel. She was a little out of sync with the pill. The second time, she drove to the drug store in a frenzy.

The Northend apartment was empty when she returned with the testing kit. Each room smelled of lavender-scented bleach. Mr Anaesthesiology had been busy cleaning. Pity that Shailesh wouldn't visit her while he lived there. That the rent was paid up for the whole year. And that she was alone.

All alone.

Paper and plastic rustled. Shook in her hands. Then ripped open with a giant roar. It hit the stream of urine. Her fingers warm and wet, holding the kit. One. Two. Three. Four.

The line was blue.

Blue positive.

Positively blue.

She knelt to the floor. Pants round her ankles. Head spinning. Heart racing. Flutter! Flutter! Finally, something good happening. Yes!

Oh God, no! She'd been drinking. The champagne at the Belvedere and that whisky in Shailesh's room. Damn him for snoring so loudly.

Damn him!

She clambered up.

It would be all right. It would be okay.

Like a mantra, she chanted it. She hadn't had much.

It would be all right. It would be okay.

All over the world babies were conceived on drink. But work and exams? Oh God! Her mother would have to stay. Shailesh had to get a job nearby. Oh God, Shailesh!

She picked up the phone. Shailesh wasn't answering. She rang Dr Cray's secretary. It was urgent, she told her.

A man's voice came through in the background. A deep Southern drawl.

"That Shailesh guy? No, I haven't seen him; he's not around much."

Her heart whooshed with panic. *Dr Cray!* Her hands shook. Whoosh! Flutter! Whoosh! Flutter!

The woman apologised. Her voice, like her nails, was acrylic.

She rang the house. Suresh picked up. He told her Shailesh was busy, with his new side job. Portering patients. They were short on staff and paying good money.

Portering! The father of her child?

Eventually she found Shailesh. He was panting, after running through the courtyard.

"No! Finish it!"

His voice boomed like thunder.

"I DON'T WANT ANOTHER CHILD RIGHT NOW! Seema is like a daughter."

A shocked silence followed. She wasn't even sure if he'd hung up.

"You bastard!"

"What did you just call me?"

"BASTARD... BASTARD... BASTARD! Portering and playing hooky. I heard from Dr Cray!"

She slammed the receiver down and rang her mother. In one breath, she told her the news and mentioned Shailesh's reaction. Then she waited in hope for the rebuttal.

But Leela Bastikar just yelped with excitement.

"My dear girl, they all say that! Then the baby comes, and as if by magic, everything changes. Just give him some time."

Mrs Bastikar's buttery words hit the spot. Maybe this was just what he needed.

A child. Perhaps even why he was drinking!

Missing home. Missing Seema.

She would leave it for a few days before she spoke to him again.

23

The Women and Children's Unit was a half mile walk from the main hospital. On the ground floor there was a gift shop, a canteen and signs in bold black letters next to the lifts: Feto-maternal medicine. Delivery Suite. Neonatal intensive care.

She was definitely out of her comfort zone; at med school she'd only scraped a pass in OB-GYN. Butterflies whirred round her belly.

Early pregnancy unit. The one she wanted. Gulp!

For the past week she had held herself as tight as a rock. Gone to work, shopped and made dinner. She'd ignored the sickness inside. Until the phone call from Shailesh.

He'd spoken of trying out for family medicine jobs; there were loads available. Strange, coming from a surgeon. She'd always thought of him operating. Not portering or doling out antibiotics. She'd said something to that effect and mentioned her scan.

But it came again. That ear-splitting roar.

"I TOLD YOU TO FINISH IT! I do not want another child."

It tore her in two.

She'd begged him to change his mind. Maybe if they both took a few days off, went up to Vermont and visited family. He'd snorted.

"I'm not going anywhere near those zoo animals! My family is in Mumbai."

Furious, she'd hung up. Zoo animals? When once upon a time, he was sat at her father's feet, begging for forgiveness. He'd only called it dowry by accident. Slimy, self-serving bastard!

And then she realised that the sickness wasn't all from the pregnancy. That stuff came and went. What stayed behind was sickly hatred. She hated Shailesh. Loathed him to the core. His beer belly and his snoring. The smell of red onions, Frangelico and Laphroaig on his breath. His insistence that he didn't want a child. That Seema was enough. All of it made her want to vomit. Bleurgh! Bleurgh! Bleurgh! AARGH!

The lady at the reception desk peered at the appointments diary through horn-rimmed glasses. 'Monisha Bastikar' wasn't on it. Monisha smiled sweetly. But Dr Tyson said she'd squeeze her in, as a favour. You know... er... colleague to colleague.

Then came the big frown. Hesitation. Dr Tyson had been called away. But there was a slot available at two o'clock. Could she wait? Of course! Could she pee now? Please, please, please say she could. Yes, but she'd have to start holding again afterwards. Fine, no trouble!

Her cell phone rang. She checked the number. It wasn't Shailesh. She answered it. A man's voice. Instantly recognisable.

"Monisha, do you remember our lunch date? I've been trying to call you. I've left many messages."

Oh God! She'd completely forgotten Saurav Das was in town for a meeting! They'd arranged it weeks ago.

"Uncle, I'm so sorry. I completely forgot… I'm pregnant."

He was like family. She could see it now, the broad grin sprouting across his handsome face.

"That's wonderful! Shailesh must be thrilled."

Silence. Pangs of pain. Deep sigh.

"Nope! He wants me to end it."

In a room of splotchy skinned women, swollen bellies and ankles, a dam burst of tears. They wouldn't stop. He'd make excuses now. Promise to call her back, hang up and then not bother. All because of these stupid, stupid tears.

"Monisha calm down! Where are you? The Women's Unit? I'm just across the way. Meet you there… in ten minutes?"

Oh my God! Oh my God! Oh my God!

It was almost twelve o'clock. The canteen was starting to get busy. Mostly mothers and babies. Bagels, rolls and wraps lined the display window. Fillings she wasn't allowed: prawn salad, tuna and sweetcorn. She ordered a toasted bagel and a mug of camomile tea. As she went to pay, a voice came from behind, adding a flat white and smoked salmon.

Saurav Das was here. The man who'd picked up her appendicitis at eleven. Saved her from choking at her wedding. *He was here!*

They found a table in the corner near the bathroom. Over lunch, she recounted her first meeting with Shailesh, the young surgeon with a widowed mother. A sister heading out to Dubai. Good exam scores. A job lined up with Professor Sawhney. Then Ayesha's divorce. Her child. The dowry. How New York suddenly became Wichita. And Wichita became Three Oaks. Where he was drinking… and portering. Not turning up. And not wanting a child.

The last bit hurt the most.

Saurav Das took a bite from his bagel and shook his head. "He never had good exam scores, Monisha. That's why Sawhney wasn't interested."

Monisha shot him an incredulous stare.

"WHAT? He told me he had high 230s. Said it to my face!"

Saurav Das chuckled. "And you believed him, did you? Did you ask to see his score sheet?"

It was a loaded question. Her mind flashed back. The Kulkarni's flat. Before the wedding. A large brown envelope labelled 'Certificates and results'.

Its edges sealed.

Like a slab of meat in a cold room, she hung. Limp with shock. The thought pierced her. *How could he?*

"He's a seasoned liar, Monisha. His practice wasn't doing well either. After a year of trying, he decided to pack up and come here."

His words rang over and over. Everything took time to process in her numb, frozen state.

"You mean it had nothing to do with me?"

Saurav Das looked at her blankly and shrugged his shoulders. He was nephrology trained. Methodical.

Meticulous. He stuck to the facts. Everything else was speculation.

Monisha stared back, unconvinced. Surely Shailesh hadn't lied about starting a life together. He couldn't have. What about the wall tile? The hand-painted sunflower, the first piece of their first house? *Oh my God!*

If that was all fake, she hated him even more. Hate! Hate! Now each cell of blood she gave this baby was packed with hate.

She belched. Butter and bagel gurgled. The sickness rose fast. She sprinted to the bathroom.

Retch. Retch. Ugh!

Nothing.

She glanced up at her reflection. Her hair greasy. Circles round her eyes. Dark and deep. Her face drawn. She splashed water on it. Aargh! COLD!

Shivering, she walked back out. Saurav Das rose to help her.

"Are you okay?"

She shook her head.

"I want to end it."

He took her arm and guided her to their table.

"End what?"

"The marriage. The pregnancy. I don't want his child."

Instantly, his olive skin turned pale. He heaved a deep sigh and sat her down. Taking hold of each hand, he spoke of his own grief. The grief of childlessness. How Swati would have given anything to be sicking up in that bathroom. Even now. How they'd spent year after year, traipsing through corridors on cruise liners to fill the space.

Hollow, joyless years.

But for herself and Shailesh there was still hope. Now that the truth was out, they could start over. Family medicine, so what? A place together. One child. Then another. Yes, the lie was horrible! People would say all sorts! But if she forgave him and he promised not to do it again. Forgave, not forgot. Eventually, three days would become three weeks, then three years. By which time it would be well and truly buried in the past.

Could she do it? Could she grab life by the horns and pull?

She squeezed his hands. Her eyes shone with tears.

"I can."

The words came out in a whisper. She nodded. Raised her voice.

"I can."

Shortly afterwards, she headed for the early pregnancy unit alone.

Everything was going to be just fine.

24

The tiny Northend flat was now packed to the brim. Mrs Bastikar had bought over a truckload of things. Massage oil, hair oil, peppermint oil, maternity clothes and boxes of vitamins. Anything that would make life easier for her pregnant daughter and cushion the aftershock from that terrible, terrible lie.

Thankfully, when the baby came all would be forgotten. According to Leela Bastikar, a new baby could instantly wipe away the past and whiz them towards a new future.

Despite her mother's reassurances, for Monisha, it seemed like every wall was caving in. The department of medicine wasn't exactly thrilled by her pregnancy news. Her colleagues winced and groaned when they found out their holidays clashed with her due date. And just that morning, when she'd asked for help, one resident had rolled his eyes at her.

"So rude! He saw me being sick," said Monisha, after describing the episode to her mother. "Like I've never bailed him out before!"

Mrs Bastikar filled the toaster and turned on the switch. She shrugged her shoulders.

"He is just worried that your work will fall on him. That isn't fair either."

Eventually, she handed Monisha a piece of unbuttered toast and wiped the worktop before lowering herself awkwardly onto the cheap wooden chair.

"Oof! I don't think it's fair on anyone – pregnant ladies working. Not themselves, not the baby." Leela Bastikar vigorously rubbed her back where it ached from sleeping on the fold-out bed. "And not on their mothers either."

They both burst into laughter. The half-hour lunch break was soon over. Twenty minutes for eating and ten for walking. No doubt some resident would be timekeeping.

The phone rang. It was Shailesh. His voice, distant. Unfamiliar.

There was an interview in Salem. He wanted to stay the night.

Avoid a hotel bill, more like it.

"My mother's here," she told him.

"When is she leaving?"

His nastiness pricked her flesh.

"Can't you be nice? What have *they* done to you?"

Leela Bastikar, who'd been straining to listen, began waving her arms wildly.

"Just leave it, Monisha!"

She looked up at her mother. Guilt ridden.

"Fine, I'll book a hotel," said Shailesh.

It was confusing. What to say now? She asked him if he'd drop by.

Silence. Stone cold.

"I'll ask around then. Maybe someone else has a room free."

Instantly, her belly hurt. Shailesh was causing proper pain now. It came in waves. Her parents finally knew about the lie, but Saurav Das hadn't breathed a word to anyone else. She had to ask, would they tell the others?

Leela Bastikar froze. Her mind flashed back to the Belvedere. Gold and silver butterflies. *My son-in-law Dr Shailesh Kulkarni. MBBS Karnataka. MS Mumbai.* Her voice hoarse from repetition.

"Perhaps it's best not to make any big announcements."

The rest of the day was peaceful. Monisha worked solidly and got home by eight o'clock. After dinner, they watched reruns of Oprah. When they finished, Leela Bastikar made up the fold-out bed. Within minutes, each was in bed.

An hour later Monisha woke. Pain throttling her. Ripping right through.

"AARGH! AARGH! AARGH!"

She reached for the light switch, but tumbled off the bed and onto her mother.

"MONISHA! Oh God!"

Warm blood trickling down her legs.

"Nine one one."

Head spinning. Fading fast.

"Mom dial nine one one."

25

The room was white, ghostly white. Walls. Ceilings. Window panes.

In front of her was a woman: Hair tied back in a band. Her face blurry white. Lifting up a chart. Looking at it long and hard.

She knew her from somewhere. Where?

From the scanning room. Dr Tyson! Showing her the baby at nine weeks. Finding its heartbeat. *Cracking jokes!*

But this Dr Tyson was different. She was speaking slowly, enunciating each word.

"You're fine… Lost a bit of blood… You've had mor-phine… but some-thing was ser-i-ously wrong… so so-rry… but the fetus wasn't vi-able."

Schmoozy woozy morphine.

A slow spaced out nod.

"Oh."

Funny how she called it a fetus now.

138

Shailesh was in the doorway. His fat, red face peering out from behind an enormous bunch of flowers: carnations, roses, peonies perhaps.

Smiling.

"I got the job."

She closed her eyes and let his fat, lying face disappear into a purple-pink peony haze.

When she woke, he was still there.

Like waves, crashing forth.

Hate. Sorrow. Hate. Sorrow.

A nurse walked in and yanked down the blinds. Sunlight gushed through. She scribbled on the bed chart and left.

For God's sake give me something. Morphine. Midazolam. *Anything! Make me a street junkie. Nothing matters now…*

"I hope you're happy, Shailesh."

Her mother cut in. Swanker was bringing the car around. They could all drive home together. If they left now, they'd be in Vermont that evening. The hospital had given her special leave.

Monisha shook her head, vehemently.

"Bereavement leave. Are you kidding me?"

She knew what that meant. Have a few days out to cry. Then return to this hell hole. The sniggering in the coffee room, the payback on calls. No way!

Shailesh walked over to her bed with slow hesitant steps. Then he placed himself on it as gently as he could. It was the closest they'd been for months.

"I'm going to come with you all and stay. I've handed in the keys to Three Oaks."

Monisha winced as the bed sank down.

"How convenient. A week ago, we were zoo animals."

Leela Bastikar groaned and cupped her ears with her hands.

"MONISHA. PLEASE!"

Her mother was screaming now. But what did she expect? An eight-hour jaunt through New England and it'd all be fine when they got to Burlington? Monisha shuffled further down the bed and tried pulling the covers over her head. With Shailesh there, she couldn't move. He was blocking her. *Blocking her!*

Tears burst out. Hot. Stinging.

"Mom. I've lost everything!"

Shailesh stood up and Mrs Bastikar sat down in his place instead.

"Right now, it feels like that," she whispered, as she lifted Monisha's hand.

Shailesh leant over towards them both. His eyes filled with tears.

"I am so sorry for everything I've put you through. Everything!"

He began to sob. His face and body shook awkwardly. Leela Bastikar placed an arm on his shoulder. A nurse knocked, opened the door and then closed it again.

"And I *would* really like a child... I just needed a proper job."

Monisha glanced up at Shailesh, then looked round the room. On one side of the bed lay an overnight bag stuffed with clothes. In the cabinet next to her were Tupperware boxes filled with samosas and coriander chutney. Her mother must have worked through the night.

She breathed a heavy sigh and forced herself to stand. Right now, there was nothing left to do but get in the car.

26

As August drew to a close, the bedrooms of the Bastikar's Burlington home emptied one by one. First Swanker left, for exam retakes. Then Monisha was summoned back to St Anthony's. Shortly afterwards, the Bastikars shot off to Mumbai, with Shailesh.

Monisha hoped he might have joined her to go house hunting. But it was the tenth anniversary of his father's death. There were sacred rites to perform. Mrs Kulkarni had booked a priest and a temple. So, who could argue?

She'd kept herself busy by form filling. Rejecting a three-year oncology placement in Vermont. Accepting a training position in Boston, even if she hated the place. Just to be closer to her husband. So that one day, hope to God, fingers crossed, legs crossed, arms crossed, they could start a family.

After her bereavement leave, Monisha was made to work Thanksgiving, Christmas and New Year. If she wanted a holiday, the others would cover her, if she took it right away. And there was only one place in the world she could just turn up without booking. With better weather and instant company.

Mumbai.

The city had been transformed by cell phones. From the camel keeper to the street sweeper, everybody had one pinned to their ear. Car horns and bicycle bells were now drowned out by the Nokia ringtone. Monisha stepped out of the airport and into a maze of advertisements for handsets, call providers and contracts.

Shailesh waved from the taxi rank. Phone-less, he seemed out of place. He grabbed her suitcase and pulled her into a waiting car. She took a deep breath. Soon they'd all be there. Mrs Kulkarni, Ayesha and Seema, swanning round Shailesh. Crammed into that cluttered flat.

The cab bumped and ground towards Andheri East. Monisha bounced upwards and landed with a jolt.

"I can't believe he can speak on the phone and drive. With one hand!"

"They've always driven one handed," said Shailesh. The dusty green-and-gold lettering of Madhav's flashed ahead. He pointed.

"Should we stop?"

Monisha nodded effusively. Anything to delay the inevitable.

The plastic tables were oily and coffee stained. But that didn't matter. She ordered their specials: pav bhaaji and carrot halwa. Moments later, the spicy vegetable curry soaked its way through the buttery bread and onto her taste buds. And the delicious helpings of creamy, sugary carrot helped her forget anything unpleasant that lay ahead.

The Kulkarni's flat had been refurbished. In front of the kitchen stood four smart leather chairs and a brand-new dining table. Mrs Kulkarni leaned in front of it, smiling, dressed in her usual white cotton sari. Chemjong had bought it for them. Apparently, he'd turned out to be an excellent son-in-law after all.

Seema burst out of a bedroom. Tall and lady like, at three years old. Ayesha, all bosom and belly now, sauntered behind her.

"Aunty, Aunty, we went to the jungle!"

"There were lots of mosquitos," said Ayesha, lifting up her arm to display a solitary bite. "I understand why you didn't want to come."

Monisha's forehead crinkled into a frown. She had no idea what they were talking about.

Seema fluttered excitedly round her mother. "You missed it, Aunty. Uncle Shailesh took us. My daddy was there and Grandma. We went on a boat, saw tigers... and we stayed in a lodge!"

Shailesh had disappeared into a bedroom. Monisha found him, curled up on the bed, with the remote control. She shot him an icy glance.

"You didn't just come here for the death anniversary."

He looked up briefly.

"You'd booked a trip... without me."

He opened his mouth to reply. But she'd already hoicked up her bags and began running. Out of the bedroom, past the dining table, through the reception room. This time she wasn't going to wait for her sandals.

Down the stairs she scurried, her bare feet gathering dust on the concrete steps. Panting. Waddling. Ayesha followed. She was due in a month.

"Monisha! I thought he'd asked you!"

Ayesha's voice trailed off into the air. She ran even faster. Like the wind, she soared. Adrenaline spurting. Bags bouncing. Her bare feet on the main road now. Stones. Gravel. Stabbing. Aargh! What did she have in her handbag? Flight socks.

That would do it.

A taxi driver stopped when he saw her outstretched hand.

"Has someone stolen your shoes, ma'am?"

She was bent double now. Shaking her head. Gasping.

"Sitara Road," she said.

The driver lifted her case into the boot.

27

The festival of Raksha-Bandhan was an annual event at the Sitara Road house, but Leela Bastikar hadn't tied the threads of sisterly love on her brothers since childhood; the ceremony always clashed with the start of school. This year, she'd been determined to host the function. After all the drama, it provided a perfect opportunity to escape to her holiday home.

When the doorbell rang, Mrs Bastikar jumped up. The Dases were in Mumbai, so she was expecting a visit. Instead, she saw Monisha on the monitor, holding a familiar Samsonite suitcase. As the door creaked open, she noticed her dishevelled hair and flight socks.

"What happened, beti?"

Monisha stared blankly and plonked her suitcase onto the swirly marble floor. Apart from a fresh coat of paint, the sitting room and dining room were unchanged. Everything seemed so comfortable, so familiar: The kettle boiling in the background. Cricket on TV. The aroma of cardamom tea. Her father and two uncles at the mahogany dining table, heads buried in the *Hindustan Times*. Week-old Rakshi threads on their wrists.

How could she tell them?

All along the whitewashed hallway were pictures from her wedding. In a trance-like state she walked past them, stopping for a moment in front of a giant one, encased in an exquisite frame, of her and Shailesh walking around the holy fire.

Seven times for seven lives.

Her mother must have spent ages in the shop. Sorting through the stills, selecting the frame. Then hanging it there especially.

Suddenly a choking feeling. Tight on her rib cage, her throat. Her mother knew about the lies. To her, the marriage was bigger.

That's why she'd had it framed in gold.

Mrs Bastikar paced up and down beside the Samsonite suitcase, frowning. Her brothers lifted their heads from the newspaper. Professor Bastikar raised his eyebrows, but it was Uncle Shyam who spoke.

"Where's Shailesh? Didn't he fetch you from the airport?"

Monisha looked at him. He was digging, digging. He knew something was up.

She should try and keep them happy.

Monisha told them that Shailesh had picked her up from the airport, that they'd stopped at Madhav's and that she'd just come from the Kulkarni's flat.

Mrs Bastikar breathed a huge sigh of relief.

Professor Bastikar chuckled. "Ah! So you just wanted to come and see us."

Monisha pulled out a heavy mahogany chair and sat down next to him. The helper placed a cup of cardamom tea and a plate of coconut biscuits in front of her. She selected a large biscuit and dunked it in. But the sweetness wouldn't take away the bitterness.

All of a sudden, the waves came crashing back.

Hate. Sorrow. Hate. Sorrow.

And the catalogue of lies, in time and date order. Beginning with the made up exam scores and ending with his trip to the jungle.

Monisha buried her face in her hands.

Was this how it was going to be? Lies, lies, lies?

After a few hasty sips, she got up and walked to the staircase. Everyone was staring now. She sprinted up the steps. In flight socks, her feet made no noise.

Mrs Bastikar tossed the half-eaten coconut biscuit out the window. Two crows arrived and broke the silence.

"Is everything okay?" asked Uncle Rohit.

Leela Bastikar shrugged her shoulders.

"She's probably just tired."

Monisha reached her bedroom. On the walls there were family photographs. Mostly black and white. Her grandparents' wedding. Her own mother and father's wedding, and Aunt Romila's. There were no wedding photos of Uncle Rohit or Uncle Shyam though; her mother didn't like their wives.

Everyone was married, not necessarily happily.

Underneath the wedding photos was a lovely picture of herself and Riya, pouring a bucket of water over Swanker. He couldn't have been more than three years old.

Family. Children! Too much to lose!

Shortly afterwards, Mrs Bastikar appeared. She drew the curtains, tiptoed up to the bed and sat down.

After a protracted silence, Monisha let the words trickle out. She told her mother about the latest lie: the family trip to the jungle, without her.

"But husbands *will* always do something that upsets you, Monisha…"

And where was the love that was supposed to have grown little by little? It hadn't yet shown itself.

Leela Bastikar screwed up her face.

"Love? That's what Americans chase after! Look in the magazines… everyone is in love, and it lasts for two minutes!"

She pointed a knobbly finger at the framed photographs lining the walls.

"But sacrifice… duty… family… these last for a lifetime."

Monisha folded her arms and sighed. When Shailesh rang later, that evening, she forced herself to take his call.

28

The first time Mrs Kulkarni rang to check up on her daughter-in-law, her voice was filled with concern. Had she reached home safely? Had anybody said anything to upset her? Was she ill?

The next evening, when she rang again, her words carried a hint of annoyance. Was the party at Highgate Golf Club still going ahead? Ayesha had gone to great lengths to arrange it, even though she was almost due. Unfortunately, only a Tuesday was available. Chemjong's client had loaned them the function room and the biryani from Dhiraj Cabin had already been paid for!

"So, sister, shall we carry on… or is Monisha still *unwell*?" she enquired.

Mrs Bastikar apologised profusely. She'd forgotten about the celebration party for Shailesh. Her daughter was suffering from, how could she put it? Mental exhaustion. A couple of days at home and a visit to the beauty salon would put things right.

"We'll bring her to the party," promised Mrs Bastikar. "With her suitcase, of course."

Monisha grimaced. What were they celebrating exactly? Shailesh was a surgeon, his exam scores weren't good enough to get him a surgical job. And he'd lied.

Mrs Bastikar ignored her daughter's whining and asked the helper to bring down the box of new saris from the attic. The young man arrived with a ladder from the garden, trailed dirt across the marble floor and received a scolding.

When the box was finally down, Monisha flicked through the collection. Mrs Bastikar picked up a royal blue silk with a black floral border and handed it over to her daughter, along with a sapphire set to match.

Monisha held it up to the light. Spools of silvery thread sparkled, bringing a smile to her face. Perhaps, she thought, unhappy marriages were easier to tolerate in India. With the pollution and the traffic, people were too busy trying to breathe and get to places. Who had time to worry about what their spouses did? And every few days a party or a festival. Nothing like a plate of biryani and a new sari to take the pain away!

The next day, the Bastikars arrived at Highgate Golf Club. The function room was decadent. Orange-and-gold striped curtains lined its enormous bay windows. On the walls hung a gigantic, sideways-glancing Queen Victoria and portraits of past presidents. Children ran along the polished wood floor, between Chesterfield suites. It was a scene Monisha had dreamed of; without the lying husband, of course.

She scanned the room for the Kulkarnis. In the corner, near the bar, stood Shailesh. His greying hair had been trimmed and dyed jet black. His belly was hidden beneath a sculpted navy suit. As he sauntered over with a glass of lime water, grinning from ear to ear, her heart began racing, but in a jumpy and unpleasant way.

"It's good to see you," he said, as if nothing had happened.

Before she could reply, Shailesh turned towards the Bastikars and hugged them. He greeted Aunt Romila with a namaskar and shook Uncle Rohit's hand firmly. As Mr and Mrs Das arrived, there were more hugs and handshakes. Uncle Rohit flashed a smile.

"Congratulations Shailesh! But family medicine? Whatever happened to surgery?"

Monisha looked down at the floor, Shailesh seemed undaunted.

"I'll still do minor ops," he said, shrugging his shoulders. A waiter came around with a tray of serviettes, toothpicks and cutlets. Shailesh grabbed a plate and passed it to Monisha.

Saurav Das jabbed at a cutlet and cast him a mischievous stare. "You'll have an easy life now... Be the one home first... You'll have to do the cooking."

Shailesh's forehead rippled into a frown.

"No. My mother's coming over!"

That was the first Monisha had heard of it! Chillies and lime niggled away at her stomach. Oh dear God... when?

Shailesh raced off to find his mother; they returned, arm in arm. Leela Bastikar gleefully rubbed her hands. Now there would be someone to cook and clean for her daughter. Mrs Kulkarni placed her bony arm round Monisha's shoulders.

It felt cold and hard.

"I must go to America! My son relies on me for everything. He won't even buy a house without me."

Monisha winced. She'd wanted to go house hunting with Shailesh. Now Mrs Kulkarni would be tagging along. Making decisions. Ugh!

After three loud claps, there came an announcement. Chemjong was asking the guests to make their way to the lunch table. Ayesha stood beside him, love handles and pregnant belly spilling out of her sari. Marital bliss etched on her face.

"Come on everybody, there's Peking duck as well!"

Monisha groaned softly and let out a helpless sigh. Peking duck was the last thing on earth she needed right now.

She felt a woman's gentle grip on her arm. Amidst the clattering of plates, someone had read her thoughts. Swati Das was calling her to their table.

After lunch, the guests dispersed into the frenzied Mumbai traffic. The Bastikars squeezed themselves into Aunt Romila's jeep. Ayesha and Seema went with Chemjong to his family home. The cab that arrived to take the Kulkarnis back seemed ludicrously small. With the gifts stuffed in the boot and the Samsonite suitcase taking up the entire front seat, Monisha clung on in the back, sandwiched between Mrs Kulkarni and Shailesh.

Thankfully, the ride to Andheri was only twenty minutes long. When they arrived, Monisha watched with dread as the same dull routine unfolded. Mrs Kulkarni handing her son a glass of iced lime water. Shailesh drinking it. Undressing to his boxers. Passing his dirty clothes to his mother. Mrs Kulkarni placing them gently in the washing machine. Pulling out a fresh towel from the cupboard and a bar of sandalwood soap, still in its wrapper. Giving them to Shailesh.

"Do you need me to do any cooking?" asked Monisha, knowing full well she didn't.

"I've made us something light," said the old woman.

Because we've eaten rich today. Blah. Blah. Blah.

She wandered over to their bedroom. On the edge of the bed lay a brand-new throw, vibrant green, on the space where Shailesh had sat the day before their wedding. Before he'd flung his turban on the floor and mentioned the d-word. Before she'd run out the door and he'd followed her on his motorbike, to Sitara Road, where the marquee was almost up. And in the front room, he'd sat, at her father's knee, crippled by debt. Begging for money. Lying about his job, his scores. If only she'd known.

If only. If only...

Shailesh poked his head in. He was going to the other room to watch TV. Did she want to join him? She looked up at his lying face and the new jet-black hair. No, she told him, but thank you. She preferred to rest.

Monisha headed for the bathroom, washed her face and changed into a cotton nightdress. Within moments she drifted off to sleep.

She was only half awake when she heard Shailesh's voice.

"COME! See this on TV!"

She took her time. It was probably one of those dreadful comedy shows. She brushed her teeth, made the bed.

"Quick! Something's happening in America!"

She ran to the other room. She was puzzled by the scene on the TV. Flames. Orange. Grey. Two planes crashing into two buildings. The twin towers. Toppling down. Like in a movie.

But it wasn't a movie.

That was New York. Buried in ash. They were New Yorkers. Running away. Soot covered. They were real fire fighters. Real flames.

Terrorists did it. Two of them. They boarded at Logan International.

Her airport.

She watched. Numb. News poured in.

Breaking news: two sentence horror-filled lines.

Other attacks. Planes again. The Pentagon. Pennsylvania.

The president was there now, standing in the rubble. Talking into a megaphone. Next to a star-spangled banner.

Her president.

Then she saw a man jumping out of the North Tower.

A hundred floors.

A pain struck her heart. She broke down.

"It's to do with America's policy in the Middle East," said Shailesh, shaking his head.

But she wasn't listening. She'd seen the jumping man.

Monisha ran to the phone and dialled. She knew the Dases were staying over. Her mother picked up. In a trembling voice she answered. They were supposed to be

154

flying out in the morning. But no flights were running. She asked to speak to Uncle Saurav.

It was carnage, he said. Carnage! He'd rang his friend in New York. Doctors were gloved up, waiting, but the casualties weren't coming in.

"They're lying dead," he sobbed, "in the rubble. There's just a smell of burning… of burning flesh."

She cried with him.

Behind her Mrs Kulkarni was hovering. Pointing at a cup of tea. Cheap, wood-smelling, Kulkarni tea.

She had to do it. It was now or never.

"Uncle. SALIR… MATRIMONIO."

"What?"

"SALIR MATRIMONIO. Will you help me?"

He told her, he'd phone her later. She knew darn well he'd understood.

They all spoke bitty Spanish.

29

The breakfast table had been laid out. Soft, brown chapattis were being kept warm in a steel-lined dish, beside a steaming pot of cauliflower curry. Mrs Kulkarni walked out of the prayer room smelling of incense and coconut oil. On the chair closest to the door, Monisha sat waiting.

It had been a night of nightmares. AK forty-sevens and Kalashnikovs. Bearded terrorists running wild. Maiming. Killing. Drilling bloody holes into innocent bodies. Then she'd been woken by Shailesh's snoring. She managed to fall back to sleep and found herself wandering through a desert, battling a harsh sandstorm, alone. A kick from one of his tree-like legs ended that dream.

Mrs Kulkarni opened the steel-lined dish, took out a chapatti and waved it in front of her. She called Shailesh. Sleepy-eyed he wandered in from the bedroom.

"I won't be eating," said Monisha.

Mrs Kulkarni looked puzzled.

"Why?"

Monisha stared them square in the eyes. The panic and fear had subsided.

Only numbness now. She took a breath.

"I'm leaving this marriage."

Shailesh crashed down onto the chair and looked up, puppy-eyed, at his mother. Mrs Kulkarni's mouth widened like a cave.

"But why? I've got a job now… Things are looking up!"

Monisha shook her head. No 'perhapses' this time.

"You never *really* wanted to marry me Shailesh, or live in America."

Mrs Kulkarni interjected. "But what is done is done…"

Monisha held out her hand like a stop sign. No one would interrupt her now.

"You love your family. You love surgery and you love Mumbai."

She picked up her handbag and slung it over her shoulder.

"You don't love me."

There was silence. For a few seconds. Stone cold, but afterwards, no longer hurtful. Calming and freeing, like the truth had found its voice.

Shailesh flopped down. His shoulders and head limp on the table. Mrs Kulkarni shot up, placed both arms round his neck and hugged him tight.

Underneath her suffocating grip he forced out the words.

"But, how do you know that things won't get better?"

The jumping man flashed before her. Monisha wasn't listening now. She picked up her suitcase and walked into the reception room, shaking her head and muttering as she went.

"Lies… Too many lies… Too many lies."

Mrs Kulkarni sighed deeply. Tears rolled down her face.

"Our luck has been very bad, son" she said, her voice breaking.

This time Monisha didn't have to run.

She was free. From the land of the free.

Free as a butterfly… as a bee.

From her cab, she watched bitchy, busty schoolgirls clambering onto rickety buses. Text books spilling out of over-filled schoolbags. Physics. Chemistry. Biology.

How would they all end up?

With matchmakers, mothers-in-law and dowries. Their fresh-faced, youthful days wasted waiting. In the hope that, little by little, love would grow. When it mightn't. Thinking that they had seven lives, when they didn't. In front of her flashed the sign for Sitara Road.

The courtyard of the house was now strewn with plants. In amongst them stood Saurav Das. Barefoot, with his trousers hitched up above his ankles. Keeping himself busy. Weeding. Repotting. He stared solemnly at the cab.

With a swing and a jerk, they pulled up. The driver jumped out, leaving behind her suitcase and a waft of diesel fumes.

Monisha walked towards Saurav Das.

"You've made up your mind then?"

A queasiness was starting. Her throat was dry and still scratchy when she cleared it. She sat down on the front step.

"Do you think I'm doing the right thing?"

He poured water on his muddied hands and began rolling down his trousers. He shrugged his shoulders. It was a matter of choice.

Monisha folded her arms. The usual non-judgemental, non-committal, physician-like answer. She looked at him imploringly. *What did he think?*

Saurav Das stared out at the passing road, at the people walking. Then he remembered his wife and sighed.

"Chronic unhappiness is like chronic pain, wrenching away at you, bit by bit till there's nothing left."

Thoughts bubbled away in his head as he put on his shoes. He scooped up her suitcase and smiled.

"You're young, beautiful. You may meet someone better."

He took hold of her arm as they made their way to the side door. Swiftly his smile disappeared.

"But there are no guarantees in life, Monisha ... No guarantees."

The door creaked open. Professor Bastikar and Mrs Bastikar were seated at opposite ends of the table sifting through bank statements and doing the sums, hoping to escape the cold in Vermont and retire to Mumbai. Each wore reading glasses. Professor Bastikar noticed Monisha and lifted up the newspaper.

"This is going to change everything. There'll be a nasty, messy war," he said, pointing to a picture of the crashing planes.

Monisha's heart pounded loudly. Saurav Das dragged her suitcase along the swirly marble floor. She waited for the scraping noise to stop.

"That's not why I'm here though, Daddy."

Leela Bastikar took off her reading glasses. Her eyebrows arched into two distinct question marks. She shifted uneasily in her chair when she noticed that the Samsonite suitcase had reappeared. Just one day after being packed into the car. Along with her daughter.

Monisha's head swung like a pendulum between both her parents.

"I'm here because I want to end this marriage."

Now her heart was pounding so loudly, she could barely hear herself.

"The world has gone MAD!" screeched Leela Bastikar. "AND YOU WITH IT."

"Mom will you just hear me out… please?"

Leela Bastikar got up from the table. She commanded the two helpers to take more houseplants out to the garden and not to return until each one had been repotted. The men walked out into the harsh midday sun. Heads down. Shoulders drooping.

Professor Bastikar buried his head in his hands.

"But why Monisha? Has Shailesh beaten you… found another woman?"

Monisha shook her head. Tears rolled down.

"Because she's SPOILED!" sniggered Leela Bastikar. "Because you've spoiled her! She hasn't learned to compromise. Vinal Verma has done far worse things than Shailesh and his wife doesn't want to leave!"

Saurav Das interjected. Monisha's case was different, he said and Shailesh had lied.

"And he'll keep on lying, Mom. He'll never change."

Leela Bastikar stared glumly at her daughter.

"Forgiveness changes people. Giving them a chance... Having children."

She flung her arm across the table. "But you're just selfish... like the Americans. You use and throw away! Use and throw away!"

Monisha recoiled in horror. Her mother could not possibly be on his side.

"But Shailesh has used me! He only married me because he needed the money!"

The doorbell rang. Professor Bastikar buzzed it open. Hesitantly.

Aunt Romila sauntered in wearing aviator glasses and clutching a giant shopping bag. "Where are the helpers?" she asked, fanning her face with an imaginary fan. "I need some water."

Leela Bastikar burst out sobbing. "Oh Romi, please talk some sense into this girl. She wants to leave Shailesh."

"Why?" asked Romila. "Has he got another woman?"

Monisha held her hands up to her face. It was because he was a liar. He'd lied about his exam scores.

Aunt Romila whipped off her glasses and stared icily.

"Well, you're the one who stopped us from finding out! If you'd let Uncle Shyam make those phone calls, this marriage would never have gone ahead!"

Monisha gulped. She remembered it now. The night at the Palamo. The walk to the toilets. When Uncle Shyam asked her if he should speak to one of his professors.

And she had stupidly, stupidly, stupidly said NO. But, surely, she hadn't been completely idiotic.

"I'd seen him operate, Aunty... Heard his juniors tell me how great he was as well as the nurses!

Aunt Romila made her way over to the dining table and helped herself to water from the jug. She sipped slowly. After her parched throat became fully moistened, she spoke, shaking her head.

"That's not how it works around here. Talking to cronies and 'yes men.'"

Amit Bastikar shuddered. After thirty years of living in the US, he'd been clueless as well. And, like the others, he'd trusted Monisha's judgement.

"We'll get a marriage counsellor, have some sessions before—"

The jumping man flashed before her; Monisha cut in.

"He won't change, Daddy. His mother is the only woman in his life."

Aunt Romila hissed angrily. She couldn't believe it. Monisha was the first doctor in the family and now she'd be the first divorcee.

"What's the point of leaving now? Three years into it, when he has a job nearby. You're setting a bad example to the younger ones."

Saurav Das winced. "Now, now, Romila. Monisha hasn't done anything wrong. Shailesh is the one who lied."

Amit Bastikar rubbed his eyes. Everything was becoming so tiresome. And now an argument was about to erupt between his best friend and his sister-in-law.

"I can't listen to any more of this," he said feebly. "You're all making me ill."

"Amit… we're Americans. Monisha lives in a society where she is free to make her own choices," said Saurav Das.

Leela Bastikar paced slowly towards the photographs she'd framed in gold. There it was. Frozen in time. The

162

moment her daughter took seven steps round the holy fire beside her husband. And now what to do? Take it off the wall? Erase it from memory all together?

She turned to Saurav Das and began sobbing. This time, hysterically.

"You don't know what it feels like… To watch your child make the biggest mistake of her life… and bear the scar forever."

Now Romila began to cry.

The rest of the day passed in hollow silence. There was not one phone call from Shailesh. No sudden arrivals. No grovelling apology.

At five o'clock, the phone rang. Everyone leapt up.

But it was Swati Das. She'd been to every travel agent in town. There was a plane leaving for Chicago at ten o'clock. If Monisha said yes, she would get three tickets. But they were being strict now. No cabin luggage.

"And if she says no?" asked Leela Bastikar.

"She'll be stuck here."

Monisha nodded. There was a job to go back to. Calls to cover. Bosses to please. Leela Bastikar clutched her chest and clunked down the receiver. Swati Das was on her way, she said. The same cab would take them to the airport.

Seconds later the doorbell rang. Again, everyone leapt up. This time it was Riya. As soon as she came in, Leela Bastikar doubled over, put her head in her hands and began to cry.

"What have I done? Why are you all crying?" asked Riya dumping her schoolbag on the floor.

Aunt Romila wiped away tears and rushed over to her daughter's side to explain things. Everyone was upset because Monisha wanted a divorce.

"Well, amen," said Riya, making the sign of the cross and blessing herself.

"Riya!" shouted Aunt Romila. "Please."

Monisha pretended not to have heard. She picked up her suitcase and walked towards the door. Saurav Das followed closely behind. They would have to leave as soon as Swati arrived with the tickets. The airport would be chaotic.

Suddenly a tap on her shoulder made her turn round. Riya's kohl-lined eyes flashed before her like headlights.

"You should try internet dating," she said. "It's the new big thing."

30

Café Uno looked different now that it was festooned with American flags. On the front counter was a fireman's hat and a donation box. The mood was sombre, the Baristas not as jokey or smiley. They took orders and cast their eyes forlornly at the box until customers dropped money in it. After five o'clock, the office workers would arrive and there'd be only one topic on everyone's lips.

From her usual table by the window Monisha stared at the men and women at the counter, inhaling the scent of cinnamon doughnuts and freshly ground coffee as she watched them. Funny that she was sitting here now, waiting for Tina. To think, just one week ago she'd been with the Kulkarnis at the Highgate Golf Club, forcing down mouthfuls of Peking duck.

Each day had spun away in a whirlwind. Blurry images flashed through her brain. George W. Bush standing in rubble and speaking through a megaphone.

Shailesh sobbing. Mrs Kulkarni hugging him. Her parents' tear-stained faces. Aunt Romila whipping off her aviator glasses and casting her the most accusatory glare.

In a frantic escape, she'd jumped on that plane to Chicago. Two days later they were stranded at O'Hare. Tired. Thirsty. Dripping with perspiration. The airport was jam-packed with desperate travellers. There were no flights to Boston. Panic-stricken, she'd burst out crying. Would the other medical residents accuse her of playing hooky? It was Saurav Das who'd talked sense into her. The situation was beyond the control of the US government. The people at St Anthony's could not possibly point a finger at her for missing work.

Eventually the Dases found a flight to Vermont and she'd tagged along like a lost lamb.

A whoosh of wind and the scrape of stiletto heels brought her swiftly back to the present. In came Tina. Her sweeping red curls were now strawberry blonde and shoulder length. She carried an expensive looking briefcase of tan crocodile leather. A little overstated, when her office was a cubby hole in the basement of the mall. She smiled, a sad, conciliatory smile.

The last time they were here, they'd had that dreadful argument, then stormed off on their separate journeys. She to Mumbai and Tina with no specific destination in mind. Three years later, the wide-open doors of the world slammed shut in their faces. America had been attacked by terrorists. And they were back where they'd started.

"Tell me from the beginning," she said, after they'd discussed 9-11.

Monisha squirmed. She ordered another coffee and two doughnuts. Her throat tightened as she recounted their first meeting. Shailesh, the successful surgeon, with excellent prospects, a mother who wouldn't cause trouble and a sister heading for Dubai.

All of it lies.

When she got to the pregnancy and the miscarriage, Tina shuddered.

"Strange, he didn't want the child…"

Monisha clasped her ears, she could almost hear his voice.

"Finish it. Finish it! I have a daughter."

"You were right, I knew so little about him, and what I found out I didn't like."

Tina took a bite of her doughnut and wiped the sugar off her lips. She looked around and smiled once more. Every person in the café was a potential client. She handed the waitress her business card.

"How are your parents?" she asked, solemnly.

"My father is very upset. My mother isn't speaking to me."

Tina nodded. She knew the Bastikars and their community, with its neat little models of perfection. This would destroy them.

"They'll come around… eventually."

Suddenly she began giggling. A sinister, inappropriate chuckle.

"So… what was he like in bed?"

Monisha rolled her eyes. Americans did only care about one thing. She played along, launching into a description of her visits to Hutchinson. Shailesh with his red cheeks and swollen belly. The array of exotic liquor at his bedside. Single malt and raw onions on his breath. His drunken snoring.

Tina squealed, like a pig.

Funny how just a week ago, there were no terrorists. And she had a husband, a mother-in-law, a sister-in-law. What would happen now?

A pain took hold of her. Cutting, tearing. Tina saw it on her face.

"Come on. I'll help you get this over with, so you can start again."

That was it?

She shook herself and tried to think of something else. What was internet dating like? Tina gulped down her coffee and shrugged her shoulders.

"Well, you can't tell them your address or phone number. It's better to meet in a public place in daylight hours. You should take a cab so he doesn't know your car. Oh and no one looks like their picture!"

Monisha's head sank onto the table. That good, huh?

"Anyhow, you should file for divorce first. And if you're filing in Vermont, I'll need some ID and proof of address."

The pain returned. Sharp, stabbing. This was legal speak.

It was going to be over.

A swarm of office workers arrived and lined up at the front counter. Tina's voice echoed in the background amidst the rippling of grey suits and ruffle of newspapers

"Are you going to stay in Boston? He's close, in Salem."

Monisha thought for a moment. It was a forty-minute drive in rush hour.

"Could he contest?"

She recalled the doorbell ringing at the Sitara road house. Then the phone. That horrible moment that her parents had leapt up, hoping it would be Shailesh, clinging to the slightest possibility that they could fix things. But the Kulkarnis hadn't been in touch. Not once.

Tina shook her head.

"When one spouse contests it can be considered an irreconcilable difference in itself."

Damn lawyers!

Monisha stared out the window. The dance hall was across the road. Once upon a time, she'd twirled round its hardwood floors with big-bottomed Mrs Bhatia. Apparently, the old woman was still going strong. The soles of her feet were like hide.

"I could come back here… I suppose."

Tina jumped up. Cups slid sideways. Crumbs scattered onto the floor.

Monisha smiled as she watched her friend, now clumsy with excitement.

"I have to, Tina… St Anthony's totally sucks."

31

Twenty-three Adam Court was just how she remembered it. Frozen in time. The tired, old, floral-print curtains hung limp. The grandfather clock chimed forlornly in the sitting room. The wooden kitchen cupboards still hid the odd turmeric stain. Monisha crept round in her slippers, opening windows and letting out the musty air.

First upstairs was Swanker's room. The walls were lined with posters of his high-school heroes: heavy metal guitarists and baseball players. On the bedside table was his school photo. Adorable! There he was with bucked teeth and his basin haircut. He looked nothing like that now. But her mother hadn't changed a thing when he'd gone.

Poor Swanker! He hated every minute of engineering school.

"Qualification! Qualification! You must complete a qualification! After that you can do what you like," her mother would scream, each time he threatened to leave.

It worked like magic; he'd reached the final semester.

And he was always dating 'some hottie'. Though he never elaborated, except to say: "You don't marry them". In a couple of years her mother would be trawling the matrimonial columns. For a good Indian girl.

Or would she? After this?

In her own bedroom hung a picture from the reception at the Belvedere. There she was, smiling sheepishly beside Shailesh. The pair of them walking under an archway of pink butterflies. Hand in hand.

She turned her head. Saw the double bed. The one they'd slept in, after coming back. From the… from the hospital. Gulp!

Her fingers shook as she unhooked the photograph. Where could it go? She opened a cupboard and found a crate of old things: a rag doll, a music box without its ballerina and a silver cat with trinkets on its tail. All from Aunt Romila.

An exercise book toppled out, its pages filled with her third-grade scrawl.

"When I grow up, I want to be a *ginacollogist.* You have to work hard to bring out babies. Babies cry a lot…"

She slapped it shut. But it was too late. Sharp pangs of grief struck all at once. Bones. Muscles. Throat. She cried out in pain. Aargh!

In a daze, she continued to her parents' room. On her mother's dresser, the ceramic brush and comb lay blanketed in dust. A telephone cord trailed out under a pile of science journals. Her father's doing! She found the receiver, picked it up and dialled the Sitara Road number. Blubbery and shaking.

Professor Bastikar answered, in a voice weakened by hurt. He'd argued with Rohit and Shyam. They should have found out about those exam scores, quietly made some enquiries. They'd only have told her what she absolutely needed to know.

Shyam felt guilty. Now they weren't speaking.

"How's Mom?"

"Gone for a walk," he said, "and still convinced you should have given it a chance."

There was little left to say, except that the Dases were well, she'd met Tina, and in a day or two she'd be heading back to Boston.

She hung up and found her father's computer. It had been a while since she'd checked her emails. Her inbox was loaded. First, she read her brother's reply to her breaking news.

"Hope it works out. Good luck with Mom and Dad."

That was it?

Then, buried under junk mail, a message from Shailesh.

Her heart stopped. She took a deep breath before she read.

'Dear Monisha. Sorry I couldn't be the husband you'd hoped for. As soon as you left, doors started opening. There's a hospital being built nearby. Modelled on the US. They're looking for surgeons, American returned. I'll stay in Salem until its finished. I couldn't live out your dreams and give up on mine. I belong here.'

He signed it 'A sad-and-sorry Shailesh'.

Even though he wasn't either.

She forwarded it to her father. To Swanker. To Riya. To Tina.

Bastard! Bastard! Bastard!

The phone rang. It was Tina. Yes, she'd read the email. No, that wasn't why she was ringing. She was inviting her out to dinner. Justin, her boyfriend of six months, would be there. It'd be better than moping round the house. All alone.

Would it be? Seeing a loved-up couple?

Tina noted the hesitation.

"Oh please! You're not the only one to have loved and lost. In fact, you didn't even love. You've just… lost. I'll pick you up in an hour."

Monisha reluctantly jumped in the shower.

La Fontana was a pretty Italian place, with olive trees in the courtyard and a small fountain. They sat outside and waited. Justin called to tell them he was running late. Monisha gazed admiringly at the picture on Tina's phone. Justin was blond with washboard abs. A hottie!

"If he doesn't propose in a year, I'll leave him."

Monisha looked up in horror.

"Why?"

"We could be running around in circles for years. And my eggs won't last that long!"

A good-looking waiter began walking towards their table. Suddenly Tina began scrutinising her from head to toe.

"Seriously Monisha! Crew-neck sweater and jeans… To a restaurant? And what's that round your neck? It's so gold, it's orange!"

Monisha frantically began tucking her chain under her shirt. She needed a new look, thought Tina. Out with the gaudy, in with the slick.

From behind the fountain, Justin appeared. Tanned and smiling. More handsome in real life. Before she stood up to greet him, Tina poked her in the belly.

"And go easy on the alfredo. You'll need to hit the gym."

32

The next morning, Monisha rang the department of oncology at University Hospital. In a trembling voice, she explained her predicament. Two months ago, she'd accepted the oncology offer in Boston and rejected Vermont's to be closer to her husband. Now her marriage was over. Had their positions been filled? Could they possibly reconsider?

The woman at the end of the phone had no idea, but she would try her best to help. Professor Davidson was around and the 'three o'clock person' had cancelled. She could certainly pencil her in for a meeting. No promises, but it was worth asking.

As Monisha stared at her reflection in the bedroom mirror, fear swept through her body. There were only four hours left to change her look. Gulp!

The mall was full of fresh-faced cheerleader types and impossibly thin mannequins. Everywhere the spotlights and transparent glass made her hips look wider. Eyes puffier. And the tempting scent of cookies and ice cream almost drove her to distraction. She scurried past each shop. Demoralised.

When she got to the second floor, a glittery sign caught her eye. The word 'DAZZLE' was written in elegant cursive script. Beneath it, a chalkboard offer: 'Shampoo, cut and blow dry, forty dollars. No appointment necessary.'

They had her. In a flash she was inside.

As the man held up her long unruly mane, she cringed with embarrassment. When he asked her what she wanted done, she froze. He pointed at her shoulders and she nodded apprehensively.

For the next hour, he was in his element. The warm lather began to relax her. She lay back, inhaling the alpine freshness, while her frizz was lovingly tamed.

Suddenly, the taps stopped running and the man sat her up with a jolt. He took her to a new swivel chair and immediately began chopping. Ruthlessly! Each time she saw a piece of her hair dropping to the ground, she jumped with fright.

He stopped at her shoulders and added a neat little fringe. Then he dried it and fixed it with mousse and spray. When he'd finished, he showed her how to wear it out and how to twist it up in a clasp. Like a sorcerer he'd worked his magic. She was beautiful.

He whisked off her cape.

"So… are you ready to dazzle?"

She beamed proudly and handed him a $10 tip.

With new hair, it was easy to find new clothes. Slimming ones. Smart ones. Sexy ones. The look was going to be European. No more sparkly bangles or purple silks. But pale blues and soft pinks instead. And she'd be sleek! Like Tina had said. Pencil skirts. Fitted waists. No silver sandals, but knee-high boots and classy heels. With stockings. Black or neutral. And always sheer.

She twirled round each changing room. Delighted!

The one place left to visit was the jewellery store. Within seconds she found exactly what she wanted. A silver chain with a clear crystal pendant. Inscribed inside it, the letter 'M'.

She'd wear it forever.

At five to three, Monisha strode towards John Davidson's office. She wore a pencil skirt, crisp white shirt and killer heels. With her hair in a clasp and a copy of her CV tucked under her arm, she was ready to dazzle.

Associate Professor John Davidson was younger than she'd imagined. He was pale and lean with sandy hair, a shadow of a beard and rugged features. A squash racket jutted out of the holdall next to his desk.

He shook her hand and caught sight of the letter 'M'.

"How can I help you Dr Bast-ik-ar?"

He offered her a seat and sat himself down behind his desk.

"Am I pronouncing it correctly?"

She liked it when someone made an effort. She told him how she'd rejected the offer of haematology and oncology training in Vermont and accepted the job in Boston to be closer to her husband.

He nodded.

"What happened?"

Her heart began fluttering.

Damn Shailesh for making her look stupid now.

"I'm getting divorced and my parents live here. My father is actually…"

A deathly silence followed. Her chain felt hot round her neck.

John Davidson rocked forward on his chair and leaned in.

"Your father is in the physics faculty. My colleagues in radiation know him."

His voice was calm and reassuring. She found the courage to speak again. She wanted to come back to Vermont, she said.

He thumbed through her CV, then stopped at page two. "You want to relocate… because your family is here?"

Trap. Don't fall for it.

"No! My father wants to retire soon… to Mumbai. My brother is in Chicago."

Her crisp white shirt was now moist with sweat. She sat up straight and took a breath.

"I went to med school here. I like the programme; it would have been my first choice."

John Davidson ran his fingers through his hair. He seemed genuinely surprised.

Really, she would choose Vermont even after working in a place like St Anthony's?

Monisha nodded her head effusively.

"Yes! Because the people there are so… They're, er… They're just…"

John Davidson smiled when he sensed her hesitation. "Such assholes?"

She burst out laughing. Chuckling. Chortling. Giggling.

"Do you have kids?"

The laughter stopped. She shook her head.

"Phew… It's not going to be as hard then."

He rocked back and forth. They were talking like friends now.

"I'm afraid all our jobs are filled."

Ouch!

Like a rag doll she crumpled. Her necklace dangled in front of her. And from it that salty, sickly smell of sweat and deodorant. John Davidson waved her CV back at her and cleared his throat.

"But you're a strong candidate from a fine institution. I could offer you a research post, salaried. And you could re-apply, next round."

She shot up, grinning from ear to ear. Suddenly his face hardened. He stared straight at her, his blue eyes steely and cold.

"I warn you, the research I do is not Mickey Mouse stuff. With me it's a PhD or nothing."

He shifted his swivel chair sideways and revealed a bookshelf filled with PhDs. Dissertation after dissertation. Leather-bound. Lined in rows. His jaw tightened. He expected her to get results and publish. If she didn't, she wouldn't make it onto the clinical programme. He tossed her CV onto the desk.

"And now that you've messed them round in Boston, you won't make ANY clinical programme."

It was this or nothing.

Inside, she shook like a leaf. She promised him, she'd do her best.

Whatever it took.

He nodded slowly.

"It'll take longer. Six years instead of three. But at the end of it you'll be an academic, a researcher AND a clinician."

A chill ran down her spine. Things were changing. Her career. Her plans.

Her whole life course. Six years? Meeting a man… having babies… when?

Fear crept across her face. He saw it.

"You're much better off doing research. No one survives in clinical oncology without research."

Professor John Davidson chuckled when he realised the double meaning. What he'd meant to say was that a career in clinical oncology without research was pretty darn depressing.

33

The newly renovated apartment was walking distance from the campus, and two blocks away from the cafés and diners of Church Street. With its high ceilings, hardwood floors, granite tops and antique brass fans, it was stunning. Her bedroom and built-in wardrobe were enormous. The power shower in the bathroom was pure heaven. Every morning, Monisha pinched herself. The space was really hers. All hers!

She would never have to clamber over Miss OB-GYN's boxes or make small talk with Mr Anaesthesiology. Any time she wanted to, she could kick off her heels and tap dance. Or Indian dance or Riverdance. Because the place was soundproof.

Right now, the misery of her final months at St Anthony's were a distant memory. The bitter Boston winter, endless servings of bean stew and that most awkward encounter with HR when they discovered they would have to re-advertise her job and re-interview.

Ha! Ha! It was over.

Associate Professor J.T.C. Davidson had thrown her a lifeline.

John Tyrannical Control-freak Davidson.

He'd sent her a range of projects. She'd chosen one she liked. But he'd decided that monoclonal antibodies were more 'up her alley'.

What alley?

And he expected the literature review to be completed before she 'officially commenced'. The whole of one chapter written up. Between dayshifts. Night shifts. House hunting. Packing and relocating. Good God!

Her parents were unable to help. Her mother announced that she couldn't stick out another Vermont winter; the arthritis would kill her. Her father handed in his notice. And when he concluded he could not afford a house in Mumbai as nice as the one in Sitara Road, he ended the cold war with his in-laws and jetted back there.

Until Tina came to the rescue, she'd been suicidal.

Shailesh sent her an email or two. He deplored family medicine. Taking the job in Salem had been a huge mistake. Thankfully, the hospital managers in Andheri had sent him a contract. The place would be up and running by the summer and that was when he planned to leave.

Just one summer after their expensive, butterfly-themed second wedding reception.

On a positive note, Tina thought that their divorce was an easy 'no fault job'. No children. No assets to split. She could wrap it up in a few months.

And the $30000 that he'd promised to pay back? The 'loan'? Tina had shaken her head.

"Oh, for crying out loud Monisha! When you've finished, you'll be driving a Ferrari!"

But would she ever finish? Lab work was slow and tricky. The equipment was not always available. When it was, you worked through the night. Then waited and waited. Three months in, she'd only done one experiment.

And it had failed. Abysmally.

Somehow, she got through the days. There were research meetings twice a week, and Latin dance classes two afternoons at five o'clock. She met John Davidson on Fridays, and shook in her boots when he asked her how things were progressing.

Still, it counted as human contact. Lab life was lonely. Worse than St Anthony's. And without parents or patients, it seemed kind of purposeless.

She tried to mix with other students. But they were nerds and computer geeks, with different time tables and agendas. She'd gone out with them once to a Mexican place in Church Street. Where the tequila had turned them weird, like e-numbers did to kids. So, she'd made her excuses and sprinted back to the flat.

Her fur-lined prison cell.

Things would only get worse during spring break. Ten whole days of nothingness. No lab meetings. No salsa class and no John Davidson. He was on vacation with his family. Even Tina and Justin were going upstate.

And now she'd spent her money decorating, she couldn't afford a ticket to Mumbai, while that conniving Swanker had managed to wheedle money off her father and jump on a plane.

On the Friday when term broke up, Tina asked her to meet at Café Uno. Monisha arrived at five o'clock on the dot. There was Tina, sitting forlornly at a table by herself, wearing tight jeans and a ski jumper; the bobble hat still on her head.

As Monisha approached, Tina removed her headgear, shook out her curls and sighed.

"I hope Justin is going to propose soon."

Monisha couldn't understand the sudden rush. She thought he still had a few months to pop the question.

The waitress arrived with two coffees, Tina passed on the hot cinnamon doughnut, Monisha grabbed it instead.

"Only four years left till my scary year!"

Monisha took a big sugary bite. What was a scary year?

"Thirty-six," said Tina. "If I haven't found Mr Right and had kids by the age of thirty-six, I'll just have to settle for Mr Right Sperm."

Monisha almost leapt out of her chair.

"What the hell are you talking about?"

Tina shrugged her shoulders. She was talking about using a sperm donor. Monisha winced and crisscrossed her eyebrows into a giant frown. She knew her chemo patients donated to sperm banks. But that was different!

"Why would you do that?"

"Why not?"

Monisha looked her friend in the eye. Wouldn't it be nicer if the child had a mother and a father? And whatever happened to falling in love and marrying?

Tina squirmed in her seat and stared wistfully into her latte.

"That would be perfect… but you don't get perfect."

Monisha folded her arms. Utter madness! There were

thousands of babies in the world who needed a mother! Millions maybe. Why not adopt?

"Bringing a child into the world without a father seems a little…" She had to be careful not to offend her best friend and divorce lawyer.

Tina stared longingly at a baby in a pram.

"I just want to go through the whole thing from scratch once. I'd adopt the second."

Monisha wiped her mouth and the sugar crumbs off the table.

"Maybe Justin will propose," she said, sounding as hopeful as she could. The rest was far too complicated.

By the time they left it was dark and freezing. In Vermont, spring was more of a concept than a reality. Monisha stared dog-eyed at Tina as she jumped into her car. Any moment now, the week of solitude would begin.

Tina groaned.

"Hey! I've had had my share of lonely vacations too, ya know."

After a few minutes Monisha was back in her fur-lined prison cell. She flopped onto the couch and grabbed the remote.

Tina's scary year was thirty-six.

Once upon a time hers had been thirty.

34

The air was riddled with the smell of rats and reagents. Her footsteps echoed along the empty corridor. No noise anywhere, except the sound of her sensible flats hitting the slip-proof floor. Thwack! Thwack! Thwack!

A man's voice made her jump.

"The lab is not available over the holidays, but the computer room is open."

She turned slowly and saw him. Twenty-something. Brown hair and piercing blue eyes.

Sensing he'd frightened her, he showed her his badge. He was supervising. She squinted hard and saw that his name was Joe Friedman. He was the archetypal college hunk. The kind that turned her into a nervous wreck. She asked him if she could use the computer room.

"Sure, I can open it up for you." He walked a few steps ahead and pulled out a key from his pocket.

He was only a bit taller than her. Under his white coat, he wore a sweatshirt and jogging bottoms. He asked her if she had a writing-up deadline.

This was embarrassing. Completely embarrassing!

Her deadline was three years from now.

"Sort of. I'm applying for oncology residency," she said.

He nodded. He was here because they paid double time to see to the animals over the break. She noticed a tiny gap in his teeth. Cute. Not ugly.

"Why is the lab closed now? It's impossible to book the equipment during term time!" she groaned.

He rolled his eyes. There were always kids doing crazy stuff and more people around to keep an eye on them in term time. His face turned serious.

"You're subspecialising? Finished medical residency?"

He seemed impressed when she mentioned St Anthony's. Her cheeks flushed with pride. The one thing that awful place had given her.

They talked for a moment, about their projects. He'd just finished his science degree. Vet school or med school? He couldn't decide. Perhaps she could help.

He opened the room up. Towards the back were bookshelves, bursting with books. The kind that no one read and no one threw away. And, in the front, were the computers. Square, flat, black. Sterile. Flecks of dust gathering on top of them. Her heart sank.

Nothing left to do but click away for the rest of the day.

Joe Friedman followed her in. Now she was alone in an empty room. With a man she didn't know and Tina's voice ringing in her head.

"Watch out for perverts and predators."

187

The panic began. Flutter! Flutter! She heard squelching noises, jogging shoes hitting the slip-proof floor. Three Asian boys tore in. Within seconds there were bags on the desk. Journal articles. Disks. A packet of M and Ms.

"Hey Joe!" said one.

When he made them all sign the register, her panic subsided.

The next day, in front of the Asian students, Joe asked her if she wanted to help feed the animals. He could do with another pair of hands. And she could give him some advice about med school.

Anything was better than sitting at a computer all day, so she agreed. When she followed him out, one of the students made kissing noises. The others began laughing.

Nerdy geeks!

Joe's work was complicated. The rats needed to be weighed, given food and water. Drugs had to be drawn up and injected. Monisha held them down clumsily and managed to get bitten, even through thick rubber gloves.

Joe was too busy to notice. Every so often she caught herself staring at his glimmering blue eyes. He didn't notice that either. It was gone two o'clock when they finished.

He invited her to the office for a coffee. On the back wall, she noticed John Davidson's picture, in the top row of faculty members. Joe rushed off for a while and returned, with a steaming mug of coffee, which was almost black.

"Sorry, not much milk... You must be pretty bored to be over here."

She froze. Tried not to answer. It was none of his business.

"Look, I hate holidays too. My folks are in Wisconsin."

An awkward silence followed.

"How about we go grab a bite to eat?"

Monisha looked round. The Asian students had gone. *Was this a date?*

Within moments, his white Toyota trailed behind her car. A flurry of white snowflakes trickled down against a grey sky.

They found a burger joint and sat on high stools facing the window. He talked about his mother, a high-school beauty queen. And his father who'd died suddenly, after an argument, with her.

It took a while for her to announce.

"I'm separated… divorcing."

This time no chill ran down her spine. No faces of Shailesh and Mrs Kulkarni either.

No finality. Only possibilities.

He made a thumbs-up sign and tossed an onion ring into his mouth.

"I've got to get back and feed the animals. Shall we catch up… later?"

Monisha nodded: a nervous yes. But where? A meal out, a drink and a club meant at least fifty $50. And she couldn't expect him to pay for her.

"Any ideas?"

She shrugged her shoulders. "I could cook you dinner… if you like."

He heaved a sigh of relief. "Phew. I thought you were going to suggest something expensive."

They both burst out laughing.

"I'll bring the beers."

She headed back to the apartment and rummaged through her cupboards. What could she throw together.

Tinned tomatoes. Onions. Garlic. Mince. Lasagne? Damn! No sheets, but there were aubergines. Moussaka! More upmarket than spaghetti bolognaise, but just as cheap. She opened the bottle of red Tina had gifted her when she moved in: Malbec. Apparently, Argentinian wine was the in thing.

The bell rang. Swati Das and Saurav Das stood eagerly in the doorway. Did she want to join them for dinner? Lured by the smell of frying onions, Swati sauntered into the kitchen.

Monisha told them she was on her way out.

"Frying mince and wearing an apron?" enquired Swati.

Her face turned scarlet. She told her it was for one of the guys in the lab.

Saurav Das butted in.

"But I like moussaka!"

"I'll bring you some… tomorrow."

Oh God! Oh God! If they found out it would spread like wildfire.

She put the dish in the oven and made them coffee. While they sat, her phone beeped non-stop. Joe was on his way. She messaged him back. Her aunt and uncle were here. Could he make his way to O'Grady's around the corner? More messages flew back and forth.

The Dases took the hint and left.

After a shower she threw on a pair of leggings and an oversized sweater, then painted her lips. She glanced at herself. Her shorter hair with a fringe. The crystal 'M' on the chain around her neck. The raspberry coloured stretch knit sweater and plum gloss, all so different.

Joe arrived at half past seven. The aroma of lamb, nutmeg and oregano filled the apartment. He stood in front of her. Smooth, clean and fresh. Under his thick, navy coat, he wore a handknit sweater, not an ounce of fat bulged from anywhere.

There was an hour to kill before the food would be ready. He sat at the kitchen table swilling a bottle of beer. They talked. About nothing really. His life in Wisconsin. What it was like having a twin brother.

She told him about St Anthony's. Its work obsessed robots, who wouldn't give you the time of day, unless you had connections.

The Malbec was making her warm and dizzy. She teetered over to the L-shaped couch; he followed her. When she dropped onto it, he edged close. His blue eyes glimmered under the fairy lights. Suddenly the Malbec began doing the talking. She told him that his aftershave was complicated.

"Musky. Seaside. Sealion."

They burst out laughing.

"Ooh, that's not nice."

He put his beer down and wrapped an arm round her. She sank into him. Head spinning. They kissed. His scent was overpowering: beer, fresh mints, musky aftershave. Their tongues locked together. His hands fumbled under her sweater, fondling her. Every inch of her oozed with pure delight.

Now she was on top of him, her tongue gliding through his mouth. His hands moving deftly to her lacy bra, then its hooks at the back. He began removing her clothing bit by bit. Kissing her neck as he went. Running his fingers through her hair.

He examined her topless body.

"Wow!"

She pulled off his sweater and played with the buttons on his shirt. Within seconds he'd pulled out a condom and they were making love on her L-shaped couch.

Wild. Passionate. Carefree.

When the timer on the oven buzzed, she led him to the table and served him hot bubbling moussaka. He devoured it.

After dinner, Joe Friedman made love to her twice more. Then he curled up beside her and fell fast asleep.

35

Everything looked so different in the morning light. Her hair was limp and frizzy. The plum gloss had vanished from her lips. Mascara railroaded down her cheeks. And in the space next to her lay a mass of crumpled sheets.

Monisha called out Joe's name. There was no answer. She clambered up and shuffled into the living room, her head throbbing. Aargh! No one there. Just two beer stained cushions in a heap on the floor, and her lacy bra.

She hobbled into the kitchen, her bare feet freezing against the tiled floor. In the sink was the dirty pie dish, which she hadn't soaked. On the worktop, a jar of instant coffee, still open. The apples and bananas in the fruit bowl were gone.

She flung opened the cupboard doors, hoping to find her emergency bar of chocolate. It was gone too.

Asshole!

Her phone beeped loudly. It was probably Joe. Apologising.

She squinted at the message.

"Thanks for a great night. Off back to Wisconsin. Best of luck with everything."

Best of luck… with everything?

They were parting words. Ending words. What the Shirkes had said, with their noses in the air. When she wasn't good enough for their son. Too dark. Too tall.

But Joe hadn't told her he was going back. Hadn't said a word! She probably wasn't good enough for him either! Too old. Too divorcee.

But she was good enough for one night.

She brushed off the pangs of self-pity. Soon she was frying bread, eggs, mushrooms and tomatoes, and inhaling the glorious scent of Italian roast. After a leisurely breakfast she began cleaning the place furiously. Wiping every trace of him out. The musky scent of his aftershave was blitzed over with lemon gel. The washed pie dish was rehomed right at the back of the cupboard. And, while the bed sheets rolled round in the dryer, she laid down brand-new floral covers.

In just under an hour, any reminder of that night had vanished. And the apartment was exactly how it used to be.

Sterile.

Now there was nothing to do. She started on another moussaka, chopping onions and browning mince. Oregano and nutmeg permeated the air once more. She rang the Dases, asking if she might pop over later.

Swati said, "Yes." But it was a very tentative yes.

Monisha spent the afternoon watching reruns of Oprah. By seven o'clock she was bored senseless. She raced over to the Dases with her moussaka. The street in front of their house was lined with BMWs and Mercedes Benzes, there was barely a space for her own car. With her casserole dish tucked under her arm she pressed the doorbell. Vinal Verma's pregnant wife answered. A waft of biryani spices filled the air.

"Ah, Monisha! It's been such a long time! Come, come! Aunty Swati is busy in the kitchen."

Her heart sank. Her stomach fell to her boots. The dreaded Saturday night dinner party. And she was makeup-less. In a faded shirt and old jeans. Aargh!

Saurav Das leapt to her rescue.

"Monisha! You've made my moussaka! Wonderful! Could I eat it tomorrow?"

Her cheeks burned hot. The other ladies rushed towards her. Poor girl, they said. What a terrible thing to happen! Shailesh didn't deserve her. Why did she look so dreadfully thin and pale? Had she stopped eating?

Silk saris in blue, mauve, pink and green were cloaked round her. French perfume shot through her nostrils. The hooks and studs of necklaces and bangles stabbed at her face. These aunty types were dripping in gold.

Saurav Das grabbed her by the elbow, talking as he went. Single malt on his breath. "Monisha is so busy with her college friends these days."

She walked along the hallway, in a trance-like state. Ravi Sinha's toddler daughter came hurtling towards her, almost knocking over her dish. His pregnant wife followed behind waving a sticky ball of rice.

When she reached the kitchen, she heaved a sigh of relief. Swati Das was alone.

"If I see one more pregnant woman, I'm gonna puke," said Monisha.

Aunty Swati stopped and stared. Glassy-eyed, speechless, motionless. Her oven gloves wrapped round a tray of samosas.

Monisha cupped her head in her hands and dropped to the floor.

"Aunty Swati, I am so sorry."

Tears trickled down her face. And turned into sobs.

Swati Das put the tray down and rushed over to lock the door.

"It's just that everyone's gone now... Mom... Dad... Shailesh..."

Swiftly, robotically, Swati Das wrapped four samosas in tin foil, then spooned out biryani and salad into takeaway boxes and corked up a half-bottle of wine. She packed them into a shopping bag and handed it to Monisha.

"You need some time on your own," she said, nudging her towards the back door. "To figure it all out. Things could get messy here... with all these people."

Monisha nodded, then slipped away quietly. Firstly, onto the wet grass and then out into the half-lit darkness of the Dases' car-lined street.

Later that night, between mouthfuls of Merlot, Monisha blurted out every detail to Tina on the phone. About how she'd met Joe. Their banter at the lab. The nerdy geeks and their kissing noises. How he'd ended up in her apartment and in her bed. Blown in like a gust of wind and disappeared, equally fast. Then the ultimate ending. Being shoved out through the garden gate by Aunty Swati.

"You have to wear a crash helmet if you want to play this game, Monisha," said Tina solemnly. "And a bulletproof vest."

36

There was nothing to kill the emptiness of the cold, dark winter days in Vermont except ice skating and hard work. John Davidson was a tyrant when it came to deadlines. Most PhD students spent their first year planning their project and learning techniques, but he expected her to finish her lab work. Completely! And he always dangled a carrot. If the experiments were done and their results published, her job in oncology was guaranteed.

It was all cutting-edge science. Antibodies targeted against lymphoma cells were incubated with lymphoma cells and ordinary human cells to see which ones they attacked. Monisha toiled in the lab, sometimes until midnight. She grew, centrifuged and plated out cells. She incubated them with the antibodies and kept her fingers crossed. When they were ready to be counted, she wrestled with the complicated cell counting equipment and looked to the heavens, praying for meaningful results.

The endless cycle of growing cells, plating out, incubating and counting was all consuming. Memories of her two-year marriage and her night with Joe were pushed to the back of her mind. And the dreams of marrying and having children quietly vanished into thin air. There were only two goals right now, both boring and dreary: to write papers and get a real job. And it was just like they said: 'publish or be damned'.

She visited the Dases once a week. Thankfully, they had taken her under their wing. Saurav Das listened to her trials and tribulations in the lab, while Mrs Das cooked her dinner and always packed her extra to take home. The Dases had caught up with her parents on a trip to Mumbai.

Her parents spoke frankly with the Dases, although they said little in their hurried phone calls to her. Apparently, they had been disappointed in their son-in-law, and they could see Monisha was unhappy. But their frustration lay in the fact that she'd refused to give the marriage a chance. When Shailesh found a job nearby in Salem, she'd upped and left for Vermont. And everyone had asked why. Leela Bastikar was always tearful.

"I just don't understand girls these days," she would say.

It was pointless trying to explain. Pointless!

To blow off steam, Monisha would visit the local ice rink and skate for hours. Gliding along the ice provided a temporary escape. The booming music, peals of laughter, and scratches and skids of skates drowned it all out. The loneliness. The tirade of anxious thoughts. The guilt.

Around mid-December, she caught John Davidson skating with his son, a tall fair-haired boy. She watched from the sidelines, sipping hot chocolate with marshmallows. Round and round they went. John Davidson: distinguished academic. Owner of a luxury mansion. Husband of a beautiful wife. Father of two angelic boys.

She began to imagine how life would have been with Shailesh. He'd never have come skating. She'd tried to teach him, once. But he was clumsy. Like a buffalo on ice. And he fell so often that he vowed never to return. She pictured his son. Pot-bellied and bespectacled. Then herself, slaving behind the stove for those vile dinner parties.

She was tucked into a corner, with her face buried in her drink, hoping John Davidson wouldn't notice her. But he waved, and when she saw him take off his boy's skates and then his own, she froze in panic.

They began walking towards her.

"I'd like you to meet Oliver!"

The boy stared down at his feet. She extended her hand. He turned away. Awkwardly.

She had to ask now: could she buy them a drink?

John Davidson chuckled and passed her a napkin.

"That chocolate looks too good to be wearing on your face."

She laughed, self-consciously and wiped it away.

"Thanks for the offer, but we'll pass. Oliver isn't allowed chocolate." He looked at his watch. "And we have to be home for dinner at five o'clock and a bath at half past six, so he can be in bed by seven o'clock."

Monisha nodded, even though it sounded completely crazy.

What a perfect match! Two people with a shared love of schedules.

The little boy began pulling him away. John Davidson threw his head back. She waited for him to ask her about the project. And tell her that he expected to see results at their next meeting. But he didn't. He just let out a deep, heavy sigh.

That evening, Tina rang; the divorce papers were ready. Did she want her to drop them over?

The panic started. The fluttering in her chest. Again, a blur of images. Shailesh with his head on the dining table. Mrs Kulkarni with her arms wrapped round him. Her mother sobbing hysterically beside the wedding photographs. In her ear, Aunt Romila's accusatory voice: *"You're setting a bad example..."*

Over. All of it. Sealed in a brown envelope. Done.

"Should I bring them over, Monisha?"

God not now please!

"No... No! I'll pick them up later. But, thanks, I couldn't have done it without you."

Tina laughed. Not at all, she said. Nowadays there was a do-it-yourself divorce kit available on the internet.

Monisha shuddered. Seven times round the holy fire. For seven lives.

All of it ending with a D-I-Y divorce kit.

37

Past the library and the laboratories was the 'nice' end of the corridor. And through the horseshoe-shaped archway were the offices of the professors and their secretaries. As Monisha made her way through it, she read the gleaming brass letters on the polished oak door: 'Associate Professor J.T.C. Davidson'. Excitement burst through her body. After months of slogging, she had results.

The door creaked open. He took one hand out of the pocket of his white coat and shook hers. There was a glint in his eye.

"I've had a look. Monisha, we're onto something."

He pulled out a bunch of articles from a set of drawers, work they'd cross referenced. Those guys were small fry. Her paper was going to be huge. Worthy of *The New England Journal*. Lymphoma was topical. It might even make the six o'clock news. That is if she could submit her findings before the Italians did.

As she sat on the plush swivel chair, the brown envelope containing her divorce papers rolled off her lap. Monisha bent down to pick it up, her eyes filling with tears. Thump! It hit her like a brick. All those long lonely hours in the lab. For a pat on the back. And a few pages in print.

But no husband – no baby.

John Davidson placed his hand on her shoulder.

"I know how you feel… The long hours, the frustration. And a divorce."

He handed her a tissue. "Um… are you divorced yet?"

She waved the brown envelope at his face and nodded, fighting back more tears.

"Okay." He turned towards his computer and began typing.

"Was it an arranged marriage?"

Monisha hesitated. He typed away in bold capitals. The words glared across the screen.

INTRODUCTION… METHODS… RESULTS… CONCLUSION.

She didn't answer his question, hoping he'd forget. But he turned his head towards her and asked again.

She fumbled through an explanation. It was kind of arranged, but they'd met each other beforehand. Blah! Blah!

"How long for, if you don't mind me asking?"

Of course she minded him asking! It was going to sound crazy. And he'd judge her. Like she'd run off to Vegas. Her words came out in a whisper.

"About a week."

She held her breath and waited for the lecture. But he only nodded. And his eyes shone with paternalistic concern. Only a week? Hers was a very different culture.

Monisha fiddled nervously with her crystal pendant.

"There *are* upsides."

"Like?" he seemed intrigued.

She rattled off her explanations: the celebrations, the silks and the food were to die for. He recollected the thrill of fiery spices on his tongue. What were the downs then? She froze. He was staring straight at her.

"The pressure… To keep the family happy."

John Davidson walked over to his bookshelf.

"To keep the family happy," he repeated, thinking of Oliver, five, moderately autistic and Jack, three and perfect.

How things had changed since his first date with Lisa. The statuesque Nordic princess who became his wife and then a mother. Who now ran around scraggly haired, in jogging bottoms. Screeching.

"Mmm… Well, here in America, rightly or wrongly, individual freedoms are valued more."

He returned to the chair and sat in front of the screen. Motionless. His fingers locked on the keyboard. Monisha waited a while before she asked her question: When did he want the first draft?

He sprang up and turned sharply towards her.

"Wednesday."

Tyrant. The absolute tyrant! The fluttering started in her chest. A groaning sickness spread through her. This would mean fifteen hours of writing. Each day! In her head, the shopping list expanded: Coffee. Chocolate. Toilet rolls. Cereal bars. Bananas.

John Davidson typed away, frantically listing key points. It was a landmark trial, he said. A game changer. A completely new approach to treating lymphoma.

She'd have to get the message across. To the worldwide readership of *The New England Journal*.

Worldwide readership.

Her heart stopped. How was she going to get the message across to Tina, who'd now left Justin and who was still reeling after that traumatic internet date with a man who said he was forty-five when he was seventy.

How could she tell her best friend that, until this paper was submitted, she'd be chained to her desk? That she couldn't accompany her on a manhunt like she'd promised.

That night, Monisha made a shaky-voiced phone call to Tina. Maybe they could both go to the comedy club another time.

"No chance, geek-face," squawked Tina. "That ass-hole ass-ociate professor of yours can wait for his damn paper."

38

Three times a week, Monisha met with John Davidson. The oak door would creak open, he'd greet her with a half-smile and they'd sit on the plush leather chairs in front of his computer. For the next half hour, he'd edit her paper and plan the next stage of her project. Most of the time he kept his eyes firmly fixed on the screen. Or his nose buried in a science journal.

But, with each passing day, something was changing. As he spoke, the graphs and scatter plots merged into one indecipherable blur. And her eyes frequently strayed away from the screen and onto his chiselled jaw line.

Sometimes while he sat, his chair would edge closer and closer. Until his trouser leg brushed her naked leg. And a delicious thrill soared through her body. Making her cheeks burn. Sizzling hot. Oh!

Lately, she'd noticed his eyes travelling down her neck.

Onto her crystal 'M'. Then along each of the buttons on her shirt.

And he'd always kept his door open, for he was forever being interrupted. Mostly by his secretary, a large irksome woman. Because 'someone important' was on the line. Nowadays, he told her that he was in a meeting with Dr Bastikar, then slammed the door shut.

Occasionally, the conversation drifted. They spoke of their likes and dislikes. Monisha mentioned her favourite restaurant was La Fontana. He preferred the rich, buttery food at Aubert. His favourite wine was Sauvignon Blanc, while she fancied any full-bodied red. He loved opera. But these days he never made it out. Anywhere.

His wife would ring his office directly. Monisha knew instantly it was her when his forehead crinkled up and his voice turned harsh. After a while, though, he'd sweeten up and end with an "Okay, honey."

This always made her cringe with pain.

One day, the phone call turned into a shouting match and he hung up with a clunk.

"It must have taken guts to get divorced!" he suddenly announced. "I'm only staying because of the kids!"

Then his face turned beetroot red and he apologised profusely.

Despite their brief chats, his work ethic and time keeping remained strict. The meeting never exceeded thirty minutes. And he always made sure that the manuscript was corrected and that her research was reviewed.

That made her admire him even more.

After weeks of writing, correcting and rewriting, their paper was accepted by *The New England Journal*. The news spread like wildfire. Within minutes, biotech companies were calling with invitations to San Francisco and plane tickets. Where the esteemed Professor John Davidson and young Dr Bastikar could jointly present their findings at the Annual American Congress of Oncology and Haematology.

Her father was ecstatic when he heard the news. A paper in *The New England Journal* meant you could die and go to heaven, he said, echoing the others at St Anthony's.

Her mother was less enthusiastic. "Are the plane tickets business class?" she asked.

Monisha said she thought they were and suddenly Mrs Bastikar whooped with excitement.

"Remember Rahul Acharya's wife, that old Vietnamese lady? She's just delivered twin girls. TEST-TUBE BABIES!"

But nothing could spoil it for Monisha. She planned a celebration with Tina, who'd also heard good news. After several painful weeks apart, Justin had proposed. And now her enormous ring was being thrust into the face of every passer-by.

Monisha suggested dinner at Aubert for a change. Afterwards they could dance off the butter with Justin and his friends, at the Blitz.

In front of the floor-length mirror in her bedroom, the girls got dressed. Monisha in a figure-hugging number, generously slit at the sides, with her hair coiled into a bun, her lips fire-engine red and her feet squeezed into gold stilettos. Tina brought over a flowing dress and a quilted, cream handbag. Mrs Wife-to-Be was definitely toning things down.

Aubert had an unmistakably French air. Snooty waiters sauntered along to Debussy's Arabesque. The service was slow. Everyone sat waiting, clutching a Kir Royale. Oblivious to it all, the girls talked. And talked. And talked. At first Tina spoke about her wedding plans. After some time, Monisha revealed her dead-end schoolgirl crush on her supervisor: Professor John Davidson, who had a wife and two kids.

From the corner of her eye, she noticed a waiter strolling towards them with champagne in an ice bucket, two glasses and a note.

"It must be from Justin," exclaimed Tina, blushing. "He's gone from a commitment-phobe to goofy romantic!"

The waiter handed Monisha the note. It was handwritten. With splatterings of ink from a fountain pen.

'From one scientist to another, warm regards, John Davidson Jr.'

Her heart stopped. He couldn't have known she was here! She hadn't said. The waiter pointed. Across the way sat John Davidson opposite an elderly gentleman. Both were dressed in chinos and blazers. On their table was an ice bucket and champagne.

John Davidson smiled and waved. Monisha stood up, dumbstruck.

The two men ambled over. The elderly man had the identical jawline. John Davidson introduced him as his father, a retired professor of geology.

Monisha froze. Her throat tightened.

"T-ina, my-my best friend. Pro-fe-ssor Davidson, my su-pervisor."

The slits on her skirt were way too high.

John Davidson smiled and nodded at Tina. She flashed him her engagement ring.

"Your prayers have been answered!"

Tina frowned and tapped her manicured nails on a champagne glass making a few shrill, unpleasant clinks.

"So, where's your ring?" she asked him.

John Davidson muttered something about rings being an infection risk. Then his father butted in. He was in town for a few days visiting family, honoured to be in the company of 'two gorgeous gals'.

All the while the older man spoke, Tina noticed John Davidson's eyes travel down from the top of her friend's hair bun, to her gold high heels, via the slits in her dress.

"You better watch out for your prof," said Tina, after the men had returned to their table when their food arrived. "He spells trouble with a capital 'T'."

Monisha shook her head, he was a decent man, trapped in an unhappy marriage.

"They all say that."

Monisha took a long drawn out sip of her champagne and let the cool, tangy bitterness trickle over her tongue before she spoke. But John Davidson's wife pestered him at work, she told Tina. She rang every few hours. They argued and argued.

Tina read the label on the bottle and hissed.

"Veuve Clicquot! So, let me get this straight. His wife is home with the kids and one of them has special needs. She probably rings him when there's a problem. She gets mad because she has to deal with it alone. And because he's out enjoying the finer things in life!"

Monisha gulped down her drink, frantically.

"But John Davidson never goes out!"

Tina shook her strawberry-blonde curls from side to side. There was no point trying to explain. She'd be wasting her breath.

"They all say that too... Let's talk about something else."

The two girls savoured the delicious French peasant food and drank the expensive champagne. As they rose to leave, John Davidson hovered near their table. Would they like to share a cab ride home?

When she saw him glance at Monisha's hips, Tina cut in. Any minute now her fiancé would be arriving, she told him; they'd be heading to a nightclub

John Davidson nodded slowly. He hadn't been to a nightclub in years. Perhaps the time for those sorts of things had passed him by. *Had it really?* For a brief moment, his face turned sullen.

Monisha noticed. Damn that Tina! She just had to spoil it!

"Just make sure you don't fall in those shoes, Monisha," he said, smiling ruefully and pointing down at her feet. "You'll be presenting our paper tomorrow."

The champagne had made her all woozy. She giggled. Good God! Falling in high heels was the least of her worries.

What could be more dangerous than falling in love?

39

The fiery orange tips of the Golden Gate Bridge jutted out through the fog. From the eighteenth floor of the Crown Hotel, the view was stunning, and her suite was majestic. Cream-and-gold jacquard curtains draped the windows. On the table beneath, stood a small carafe of rosé and a crystal bowl, laden with exotic fruit. The super-king-size bed was plumped up with feathery pillows. As she flitted across the room, her shadow bounced along behind her. All this and no one to share it with.

Absolutely no one.

The first day had flown by. They'd touched down at nine o'clock, her, John Davidson and three pharmaceutical representatives. From the arrivals hall, they were whisked into cabs and driven off to a two-hour meeting. Then they were carted off to an upmarket sandwich bar, where Monisha was offered speaking engagements. John Davidson had whispered in her ear.

"You could dine out on this for a long time."

They'd returned to the jam-packed conference hall, where people scattered to attend a myriad of meetings. The pharma reps disappeared. John Davidson had taken her cell-phone number and rushed out to a lecture. And she'd found herself sitting through a presentation from a Japanese group, not understanding a single word.

At half past three, her turn finally came. There she'd stood, on the podium, before hundreds of shining faces. She could hear it now: the crackling of the microphone and the throat clearing and coughing as her pinky-purple microscope pictures flashed by on the enormous screen.

Looking back, it was such an anti-climax! Her paper was one of thousands. Her ten-minute slot had come and gone, swiftly. When she'd finished, John Davidson had simply shaken her hand and vanished into the crowd. Then, in place of the adrenaline rush, came a bleak, pervasive emptiness.

She'd wandered aimlessly amongst the hordes of delegates and made a wrong turn into a hall lined with posters. Fortunately, she'd bumped into a pharma rep. Dinner was at half past seven, he told her. They were meeting in the foyer. After an hour or so of reading the dreary abstracts, she was back in her room.

Monisha ran a bubble bath and soaked in it. She bit into a Belgian chocolate cookie, hoping that the sugar rush would be a substitute for the empty feeling. Two bites later, her cell phone began ringing. She climbed out of the bath, dripping suds onto the marble floor, but by the time she got to it, it had rung off. She shrugged her shoulders and wrapped herself in a towelling robe. It was probably her father.

When she picked up her phone and listened to the message, her heart skipped a beat.

"Monisha! It's John. Just wondered if you wanted to join me for a predinner drink? I'll be down at Rosie's Bar at seven o'clock. See you there... or with the others at half past seven. Bye."

Monisha listened to the message once more. All morning they'd sat, sandwiched in amongst pharma reps, discussing their study and agreeing to speaker meetings. He'd been remote and professorial. But now he sounded different. Calm. Chatty. Oh God! She had just twenty minutes to style her hair, change into her cocktail dress and do her makeup. Twenty minutes!

The heat from her hair straighteners burned through her head, into her body, down her legs. What the hell was happening? Was she crazy? He was married!

But unhappily. Like she'd been, once.

She curled her lashes with thick mascara. A smoky-eyed whore stared back in the mirror. Who was that?

Surely one drink wouldn't hurt!

Her cell rang again.

"Daddy! I can't talk right now. I'm off to dinner with the reps. Everything went fine."

She was lying already.

The sequins on her low-cut cocktail dress shimmered under the mirrored ceilings. She strode into the lift, a silver clutch tucked under her arm. Her heart beating against it. A whooshing thrill rushed through her as they descended. Oh God! Oh God!

He was sitting at the bar, wearing a cream shirt with the top buttons open. The creases on his forehead had melted away. When he saw her approaching, his chiselled jaw dropped an inch. Rock-and-roll drums beat loudly.

"You're late," he said, pulling up a high stool.

She could barely hear him.

"I was in the bath, so I got your message late," she replied.

He blushed.

"Nice hotel," he said, trying to shake the image of her naked soapy body out of his head. "What would you like to drink?"

Her mind went blank. She raised her eyes. Red wine on an empty stomach would go to her head. A beer would be unladylike. What to order? What did they drink in the movies?

He looked at his watch, only fifteen minutes before the others would be down in the foyer. Fifteen minutes of alone time.

"Gin and tonic please."

He handed her a bowl of salted nuts. Was she hungry? So *fatherly*!

He sipped his beer quietly and pulled his stool closer, until they were almost touching. Inside, she felt the heat of the gin against the cool sharpness of the ice cubes and tonic, and, in the background, a bitterness.

If you were falling for a married man, gin and tonic was your drink.

Their time was up. He told her to go on ahead to meet the others. He had to say goodnight to his boys.

Reality reared its ugly head. Moments later they were huddled in with industry people. He was Professor John Davidson again and Monisha was just one of his many research students. He kept his distance, joined in the conversation now and again. They discussed films and their favourite songs. His was one of Bob Dylan's.

"That song's about leaving a woman, isn't it?" somebody asked him.

Professor John Davidson laughed. Monisha looked away.

When dinner was over, they all headed for Rosie's Bar. He left the group, making the excuse that he was turning in for an early night. After one drink, she thanked the reps, yawned and said the same.

The corridor that led to her room was dimly lit. She kicked off her silver stilettos and carried them, feeling the softness of the carpet under her toes as she went. When she arrived at her door, she couldn't believe what she saw.

John Davidson was standing leaning against it.

He gathered her up and kissed her passionately. They lingered together for some time. Lips locked. Smooching. Seconds. Minutes. Her shoes dangling in one hand. Her hips sliding like waves, between his trouser legs.

Suddenly, she pulled away, tapped the card into the slot and opened the door. Her suite sprang into view. The super-king-size bed and feathery pillows. Her makeup bag, half open. The untouched bottle of rosé.

John Davidson looked shell-shocked.

"I can't do this to you, Monisha. You're too smart. Too beautiful. Too vulnerable."

She stumbled into the room, alone, and fell fast asleep.

40

The next year her research was far easier. She knew the rules and booked the equipment early. The lab work flowed. Their second paper was accepted; a third was in the pipeline. And her meetings with John Davidson were conducted several times a week. At her apartment.

Their routine was cosy and discrete. She left the lab by half past eleven and rushed back home to shower and change. At twelve o'clock he told his secretary he was going jogging. Ten minutes later, he arrived at her door, all sweaty in his running gear. After he washed, they made love. By one o'clock he was ravenous.

She'd tease him. Hide grapes and strawberries on her body, and make him find them with his mouth. When his lips tickled her crevices, she'd screech with pure delight. As he tasted her flesh, she orgasmed. Over and over again. OOOH!

And only after he'd satisfied her completely would she get up and make him a sandwich.

They knew each other's stories now. He told her about his idyllic childhood and university life, where he'd met Lisa. And how they'd fallen in love and been happy. Until they found out that Oliver was autistic. She was carrying James at the time. Then post-natal depression hit. A ruthless double whammy.

She told him about the ramshackle house on Sitara Road and her family's visits to chaotic Mumbai. About life in twenty-three Adam Court. The weekly dance lessons and dinner parties. How her mother had hunted down the perfect Indian husband. Who'd turned out to be a perfect liar.

Often, in a fit of insecurity, she'd stare into his eyes, run her fingers through his stubble and ask him if he still loved Lisa.

"I don't love the woman she's become," he'd say.

She'd imagine a beautiful, buxom blonde. Sucked away by the vortex of motherhood.

Then it would hit. Like a herd of stampeding bulls.

Choking, crushing guilt.

When he saw it, he'd wrap his arms round her shoulders and kiss her neck. Tell her she was beautiful and charming. A breath of fresh air, after his painful past. That he wanted to be with her. Forever. But he'd have to extricate himself from his marriage first, gradually.

Gradually?

When she heard that, her throat would tighten and she'd arch up, like a cat. Claws at the ready. Forcing him to leap off her and collect his things.

By half past two, she was back in his office, where the oak door was now wide open. Their meeting was brief.

The conversation was work-centric. Cold and clinical. So his pesky secretary could walk in anytime and not suspect a thing.

Even though she remained little more than his 'dirty secret', it was a small price to pay. Invitations rolled in to speaker meetings, product launches and conferences. Her bank account swelled. They spent weekends away in New Orleans, Toronto and Chicago. Eating in small groups at fancy restaurants or holed up in plush hotels.

And she seemed quite content with the arrangement. Apart from plane trips and cash gifts, he'd help her in other ways. When she couldn't locate her landlord, he mended a leaking pipe. When one of her tyres blew, he put on the spare. He even took time out one Sunday to wall mount her new flat screen television. In fact, John Davidson tried his damnedest to make up for what he couldn't give her: validation.

But, into the last year of her PhD, she began to grow weary. She was annoyed at having to creep around and became bored of listening to his grandiose plans of becoming departmental head or taking over the medical school, when he'd made no plans to leave his marriage.

NO PLANS WHATSOEVER!

Who could blame him. Once or twice he'd mentioned it and the logistics sounded grim. Lisa would get a hefty pay out and keep the house. He'd have the boys alternate weekends, even more if he could. Monisha would be the main breadwinner. And she'd have to look after his kids. Thinking about it made her stomach churn.

The images that flashed before her had been unsettling. Unruly children, she wasn't allowed to discipline. A dark-skinned half-sister they hated. How would her family react? Oh dear God! Her mother!

When the invitation to Tina's wedding came, the truth hit home. Her friend had been so busy planning her nuptials, they hadn't seen each other for months. Now she was going to be married, while she herself would remain non-validated. In limbo.

Perhaps it was better to be a second wife, than not be a wife at all.

It was a beautiful summer wedding. The service took place in Montpelier, at a quaint little Episcopal church. The bride and groom rode round in a 1925 Model T Ford. Monisha floated along behind them with the other bridesmaids, in lilac taffeta, fighting back tears.

Swanker took on the role of her plus one, reluctantly.

"Seriously, Neesh," he said as they made their way over for lunch, "If you don't find someone soon, Aunt Romila will put your profile on Shaadi.com."

Monisha gulped hard. The marriage website. God no!

She looked round the room. Each table was packed with chattering guests, tucking into bread rolls and sipping wine. Amongst them, heavily made-up women dressed in trouser suits. In elegant, but unexciting colours, such as cream and grey. Nothing like an Indian wedding, but quietly sophisticated. She smiled sheepishly.

"What if I *have* found someone?"

Swanker rolled his eyes. "Well, why isn't he here then?"

Monisha unfolded a serviette and placed it on her lap. "What if he's not quite ready?"

A glowing Tina swooped down on them. Veil gone.

Strawberry curls tucked under a cherry-blossom flower crown. Ears pricked up.

"You're still with that supervisor of yours, aren't you?"

Monisha's face turned pale with shock. She'd kill her! Kill her! In the mid-afternoon sun, Tina's flower crown shone like a halo.

"Been there, done that. Let me tell you. It always ends in tears."

She pointed her clear-varnished finger at Monisha.

"And they won't be his!"

Swanker looked puzzled. Monisha stood up and began walking.

"I need to use the ladies," she said.

Tina called out from behind. The champagne was well and truly in.

"That's exactly what you need to do. Walk away. Just like that!"

Monisha wobbled passed the seated guests. Eventually, she found the disabled cubicle. In the floor-length mirror, she saw her lilac taffeta dress, now all crumpled. Clumps of black mascara trickled down her face.

"He needs a timeline," she told herself, wiping her eyes.

"A timeline… then an ultimatum."

41

The Burlington sky was a deep, dark grey. It was gone four o'clock when they landed. The twenty passengers clambered out into the bitter wind. Amongst them John Davidson, Monisha, an oncology resident and a company rep, each clutching their laptops and weekenders. It had been an eventful few days in Philadelphia. Now they were anxious to get home.

At the conference, John Davidson had been grilled about one of his papers. A rival research group questioned his findings. They were nasty. Combative. And to rub salt in the wound, later that evening, Monisha had delivered her ultimatum.

She didn't want to completely end things, but he'd have to hire a lawyer and move out. Perhaps they could keep it platonic. Sex was becoming a chore. A hurtful, resentment-filled task, which left her feeling wounded and trapped. Like an injured bird.

But he couldn't be platonic! He told her that he needed to make love to her, be close. Feel her warmth. That he'd slept in separate rooms to Lisa for years.

Then she'd punched him. Delivered a useless girly punch. On the arm. Even when she'd used all her knuckles he hadn't flinched.

So, she ran out on him and spent the next day at the movies. Crying along with Meryl Streep and Sandra Bullock. Thoughts whirling round her head, like clothes in a wash cycle. What would the lawyers advise? What if he didn't leave?

Her thoughts spun out of control. What if she stayed his mistress forever? Like one of those women in the magazines. Creeping around in dark glasses and a camel coat. Caught sneaking out of a hotel. Hiding behind a Hermes handbag. Oh dear God!

When she saw him next, he was teary eyed and remorseful. He'd made an appointment with a lawyer. And he was looking at rentals. But they couldn't go public until her PhD was awarded and after her interview for the oncology job. That way he couldn't be accused of favouritism and she wouldn't lose face.

Finally, a result.

Previously, when she'd returned from conferences, there was anguish. A sudden realisation that the party was over and that real life would start, any minute. But, on this occasion, she felt hopeful. She strolled into the arrivals hall with confidence. A few more months of hardship and she'd be with the man she loved. Out in the open.

Who cared what anyone thought.

She knew the parting drill. The four of them would collect their luggage, shake hands and say their goodbyes. John Davidson would be driven home by the pharma rep. And she would make her own way back. Usually by taxi, but, because it was such a short flight, she'd brought her car.

Monisha cleared away the ice, and started it up. She let the engine run a little before inching out of the car park. As she hit the highway, she pondered the emptiness that lay ahead. In just twenty minutes she'd be back in that fur-lined prison cell. Alone once more. Sprawled out on the L-shaped couch, clutching a glass of red. At only half past five.

Minutes later, sirens were screeching. Red and blue lights flashed and glared. A tow truck hovered by the road side. Two men in high visibility jackets were pulling out a stretcher.

"She's walking," shouted one paramedic. "I saw her walk out of the car!"

"Amazing!" said the other running over. "Ask her something."

Monisha didn't hear the first question. Her head felt heavy, her foot prickly. It was her right foot and on the side of her face, something was stinging. Utterly uncomfortable. She gently placed one hand over her temple and felt shards of glass.

"Where were you headed, young lady?" asked the man.

In the half-light, she could just about make out a trail of spattered blood along the crisp snow.

"Home," she replied and fainted.

She woke in a hospital bed. A nurse, middle aged and Hispanic, mentioned an accident and told her that she'd had a head scan. It was fine. There were minor cuts and bruises, and she was concussed. But that was all.

"Lucky escape my dear!" said the lady.

The other guy was on life support.

What other guy? Some teen drag racer, who'd almost killed her.

Bastard!

"Is there any one you'd like me to contact, Miss Bastikar?"

Monisha looked her straight in the eye. "Professor John Davidson."

"Did you want to make the call or shall I?"

Her right hand was bandaged. Monisha found the phone and scrolled down to his name. She pressed. No answer. Straight to voicemail.

He was with his family!

"Did you want to try again later?" asked the nurse.

She told the nurse her battery was dying, wrote his number down and asked her to ring it from the front desk. If it was the hospital, he'd pick up for sure.

The nurse called her over when he answered. Monisha hobbled up. Her feet and face still prickly. Her back, neck and legs were stiff with pain.

"Hi John."

"How can I help?"

His voice was unrecognisable. Like an imposter speaking. She told him she'd been in an accident, that a teenager came at her from the wrong side of the road, and that the airbags had saved her life.

He interrupted her, the imposter.

"Okay, I'll ring you back when you have the results. Thanks for calling."

What?

He was gone.

A few minutes passed, then an hour. Then two. There was no phone call.

At half past eight came a text message.

"Needed at home."

What? That was it?

Frantically, she rang Tina. It went straight to voicemail.

With a heavy heart, Monisha decided to call Saurav Das.

42

Outside there was a hive of activity. The night staff were arriving. Keys rattled. Patient files flipped open and shut. A group of nurses spoke amongst themselves in lowered voices. Then the door to her cubicle flung open and Saurav Das burst in, wearing his white coat. He'd been in another ward, on call. He rushed to her bedside, sweat streaming down his face.

"I won't hug you," he said. "It must be agony."

He paused to look at her cuts and scratches.

"I won't tell your parents either. They'll only worry."

After asking her some questions about the crash, Saurav Das set to work. He contacted the witness and rang the insurance company. When the phoning was done, he left the room and returned with two plastic cups, hot chocolate for her and coffee for him.

All of a sudden, he sat down and looked her square in the eye.

"Monisha, there have been rumours going around. Wild rumours. About you and John Davidson."

Monisha turned her head. She could still feel the weight of his stare, hear the loud slurping noise from his coffee.

"Are they true?"

Monisha looked down at the hump in the bed clothes, where her feet were. Her eyes transfixed. The starched white sheets were cold on her legs.

Saurav Das sighed, deeply.

"I know, with everyone gone, you've been lonely… and their eldest child's condition must have taken its toll."

He caught sight of the expensive looking handbag on the bedside table. One of those designer pieces, the kind that Swati would nag him about. It made him slightly uncomfortable.

"Are you going to be the one to break up his family?"

God how did he know all this? Plain, downright nosy! She crossed her arms.

"His marriage was over before he met me."

Saurav Das leapt up from his chair, with such force, that its legs began to wobble.

"Young lady, there are a couple of things you need to be aware of. Firstly, Professor Baxter could stop you from getting the oncology job if she finds out."

Monisha shot him a disbelieving stare and shook her head. She couldn't possibly do that; the research had produced a paper published in *The New England Journal.*

Saurav Das wagged his finger. "Don't be so sure of that! Susan Baxter is a very powerful woman. And you know she's Lisa's cousin."

Monisha cringed. This fact had been conveniently omitted. Saurav Das cleared his throat, sat back down and shifted the chair closer.

"Swati handles Lisa's accounts at the bank. Last week she mentioned moving to Denver. There's a special school there for Oliver. And her own family live close by."

Monisha buried her head in her hands.

"Surely, she can't just move?"

Saurav Das stared at the crumpled bedsheets then at Monisha's cuts and bruises. His voice softened. Apparently, she wanted Oliver to start at the school as soon as possible.

"Denver University has just advertised for a new dean. She's no fool, Monisha. And why do you think she told Swati all this?"

Monisha looked up at him blankly. Saurav Das frowned deeply as he waited for an answer. When none came, he shot her a bewildered stare.

"Because I know you!"

A nurse arrived with painkillers and a glass of water. Within minutes everything was deadened. She was numb. Frozen. Her legs. Her lips. Her tongue.

Saurav Das leant over and took her unbandaged hand.

"Monisha, this accident was a message from up above." He raised his eyes towards the ceiling.

"You've been given a chance. Be strong… Walk away."

She was still frozen. A statue, made of ice.

"Time will heal."

Monisha tucked her chin into her chest and began sobbing.

The next day, back at her apartment, the curtains and blinds remained unopened. Blackness was everywhere.

Outside and in. Once or twice she got up to use the bathroom. Dizzy from painkillers. Her ribs and muscles throbbing. The pain in her chest. Crushing.

At lunch time, Tina arrived with bagfuls of groceries. First, she pulled out onions and celery to make soup, and then a giant chocolate fudge cake. Apparently, the decadent swirls of ganache icing did wonders for a broken heart.

But Monisha didn't even want to look at it, let alone taste it. She lifted her hands to her mouth, but it was too late to hide her quivering lips. Tina rushed over with outstretched arms.

"I know... I knew it all along."

Now that she was unconstrained by the thin walls of a hospital cubicle and the fear of nurses swooping in, Monisha began sobbing. Hysterically.

After handing her a giant tissue box, Tina swiftly headed for the table. There she laid out chicken, onions and a fresh bunch of thyme.

"It's nice for a girl to feel special and get all the lovely presents... without having to do the messy stuff... like bleach out the stains on his underwear."

Monisha held her sides together so it wouldn't hurt to laugh. Tina began chopping, swiftly.

"But they want it all, Monisha. Christmas and Thanksgiving with her and the kids. New Year's Eve with you."

Tina didn't blame John Davidson, even if it had been awkward seeing him in Aubert. Tongue hanging out. Drooling with lust. And she could understand why marriages fell apart when a child with special needs came along. Or any child for that matter. She worked in family law. She saw it every day.

"Sometimes, we women get so taken in by motherhood… we forget the men."

After an hour or so, Tina gave her a bone crushing hug and got up to leave. Right now, she was needed at the office, but she promised she'd be back to sleep over. The first night alone was always the hardest, she said. And dangerous, when there were sleeping pills and painkillers round.

At exactly five o'clock, the bell rang. Monisha woke with a start. She eased herself up off the sofa, then slung her dressing gown over her pyjamas, wincing with every jolt of pain. Each movement seemed to take for ever, her arms and shoulders felt like iron pillars. Eventually she limped over to the front door.

Through the spy hole, she could make out the blurry outline of John Davidson. She stood in stunned silence, watching him. The tall, creepy shadow of the man she'd loved once. Now she was thankful for the solid oak door that stood between them.

A moment passed. The bell rang again. Hesitantly, she unlocked the chain. His eyes immediately fell onto the cuts and bruises on her face. He winced and hastily extended his arms towards her shoulders. Monisha groaned and pulled away.

"I hear Lisa is moving you all to Denver," she said frostily.

He began removing his coat, like in their lunchtime ritual. Suddenly, he stopped.

"Who told you that?"

Monisha tightened her lips. It was some time before he concluded that his question would not be answered.

"She's been saying that for years. Her family is there."

Monisha hobbled into the front room and laid herself back down on the couch. When he saw there was no space for him, he began pacing. Right in front of her.

"What about the school for Oliver?"

He recoiled in horror. "Who told you?"

Monisha turned her face away and switched the table lamp on. In the soft light, she could make out that his eyes were filling up. He said he knew about the school, but he didn't know she'd put his name down. Or that now he'd finally got a place.

Monisha folded her arms and sat up.

"I don't believe a word you say."

He sank to the floor and placed his hands on her knees. Once more she felt his touch through her pyjamas; a comforting warmth.

"I haven't lied to you, Monisha. I've always said the boys come first."

Monisha put her hands over her ears. Ugh!

"Then when are we going to stop playing this silly game?"

John Davidson got up and began pacing again. Back and forth, in his coat.

"Lisa must have found out… Maybe it was you who let the cat out of the bag!"

Mustering up every bit of her energy, Monisha stood up and grabbed him by the arm. Words spurted out, like poison.

"I certainly didn't use my research fund to pay for a suite at the Ritz Carlton."

All of a sudden, she was drained. Bent double. Her voice fell to a whisper. He hadn't even told her that Professor Baxter was a relative. John Davidson gently walked her over to the couch. He placed a cushion behind her, kneeled beside her and held her hand. Tears rolled down his reddened face. "I've tried to protect you... Worked hard and helped you write those papers. Anyway, it's no use..."

Monisha began to cry. Bruised, battered and blubbering, she reached for the box of tissues, next to the half-eaten plate of fudge cake.

"When are you off to Denver then?"

John Davidson held a tissue in front of her nose and asked her to blow. Just like he did to his boys.

"Monisha, I am completely shaken up by all this too. I love you."

He placed his head on her lap and cried. His tears soaked through her pyjamas.

"But I'm torn. You're young and smart. You'll go places. But my son, he's not as... blessed, and he deserves a chance."

He clutched his chest and sobbed louder.

"And I've got to give him it, Monisha. This is killing me, but I've got to. I mustn't lose sight of that. Please, please, please understand!"

Her heart began to melt. They hugged each other and kissed briefly. A painful, passionate kiss. Then he pulled himself away and began walking towards the door. He told her he'd be applying for the chair in

Denver and that Susan Baxter could take over as her supervisor.

She stared at him, stone-faced.

"Perhaps this is best for everybody."

The door shut behind him. When she heard the sound of his car engine, Monisha reached for another round of painkillers.

43

When the snow was crisp and powdery, Burlington looked picture perfect. A winter wonderland, blanketed in white by day, festooned with glittering Christmas trees and twinkly fairy lights by night. But the black ice and gloom came a day later. First on bridges and gullies, then on the roads. With the insurance money from the crash, Monisha had bought herself an SUV. But, right now, she was terrified of driving it. Terrified!

By nine o'clock, the roads were deserted. Inside, the houses were so warm that people would literally dry up, their skin wilting like dead leaves. But the loneliness was bone chilling, and far more treacherous than the weather. At night, when Monisha climbed into bed, wild thoughts spun round her head. She wished that John Davidson's marriage was completely shattered. That the hatred between him and Lisa was so poisonous, that he'd been demoted to a 'weekend dad.' And so he was begging to come back.

In her dreams, she saw him. Dressed in his freshly pressed suit. Holdall and laptop in hand. They'd be checking into a hotel. Or sipping wine at a pharma dinner. Legs touching beneath the table. Ooh, the thrill!

Then something inside would tell her that it wasn't real. And an invisible force would prise her eyes apart which such power that she woke. Shivering. Gasping.

Crushed.

Wishing the entire world would be wiped out in an instant.

Eventually, she'd wander into the kitchen. Turn on the coffee maker. Wait for the intense aroma of roasted beans to infuse her senses and bring her back to life. But the pain was so deep it blocked everything. Taste buds. Nostrils. Everything.

It was all hopeless. There was nothing left to do except pull on her snow boots and fight her way through the blistering air and black ice to the library.

Susan Baxter was always too busy to meet. Corrections on the thesis flew back and forth by email. Her own suggestions were scattered through the text in silly looking balloons. And passages that had been painstakingly constructed by John Davidson were struck through with bold red lines.

Each week day, Monisha would sit in the computer room and type away on the old keyboards for a couple of hours. She'd attend seminars she didn't need to, and lab meetings that were now irrelevant. Just to pass the time and kill the loneliness.

When Swanker rang up, jobless and penniless, asking to stay at her apartment, rent free, she leapt with joy. Two days later, when he arrived, the pain lifted somewhat. And the good old days were back. Sipping hot chocolate with marshmallows. Skiing and skating together. Watching hockey at the stadium. With big sister paying for both of them.

With her PhD finally complete, the oncology interviews were a total anti-climax. She was a shoo-in. Susan Baxter asked her only one question: with her credentials, why was she sticking around in Vermont? Why wasn't she aiming for Sloane Kettering or Hopkins?

Faces flashed before her. Tina. Justin. Swanker. The Dases. Leave them all behind and start over? Embarrassingly, she'd choked up.

"No, no, the green mountains are home."

It had made her sound more like Heidi than an aspiring oncologist.

New Year's Eve was wild. After a drunken karaoke session, with Swanker's friends, she returned to her apartment. At three o'clock, she was awoken by the sound of a woman moaning and table legs bashing against the floorboards.

She crept out to investigate and was horrified by what she saw. Her brother's bony behind. And a woman, with a bright orange afro, like a clown. Naked except for nipple tassels. Legs akimbo on the kitchen table.

"WHO THE HELL IS THIS?"

"That information is on a 'need to know' basis," said Swanker.

Monisha let out an almighty roar and came charging towards them. The clown woman grabbed her overcoat and dashed out through the front door. Swanker pulled his trousers on and lit up an unauthorised cigarette. Beer and nicotine wafted onto her face.

"You're just pissed off cos you're not getting any, now that married lover boy's gone."

Cigarette ashes were stock piling on the floor. Monisha picked up a mop as if to clean them. Instead she waved it in front of Swanker and began chasing him round the flat.

"AND YOU BRING HOME KOOKY, FREAK-SHOW WHORES!"

Swanker zigzagged in and out. Bare chested and bare footed. Through the kitchen. Into her bedroom. Into the bathroom. Monisha followed him with her mop, swinging and missing.

"If Mom finds out, she'll stick you on Shaadi com," cried Swanker.

"And you!"

Suddenly, there was silence. Nobody wanted to go on Shaadi.com. Monisha dropped the mop and threw Swanker his t-shirt. They slapped hands high in the air and down below. Truce!

Their secrets were safe. Just like old times.

She poured out the rest of the champagne. It was flat and warm now. Swanker flicked on the Indian channel. The Holi scene from Silsila was showing. Vintage Bollywood! A lovelorn Amitabh Bachchan danced suggestively with beautiful Rekha, while their spouses watched helplessly from the side lines.

"*Ranga barse bhige chunarawali, ranga barse,*" sang Monisha and Swanker as they danced round the room in circles.

As the colours shower down, the girl's dupatta gets wet.

Round and round they went.

Just like old times.

When news came out that the PhD ceremony was in May, everyone in the faculty expected John Davidson to show, even though he was the dean at Denver. They'd given him space on the platform and invited him to the graduation dinner. In place of him, they were sent a forwarded email.

In it, he congratulated everyone who had completed their thesis. He said that he missed his esteemed colleagues and he wished everybody well, but after that he apologised. Due to other 'pressing engagements', he was unable to attend the ceremony.

Reading the email was like picking through ice. Underneath an alphabetical list of collaborators that he wanted to 'acknowledge especially', Monisha found her own name. Sandwiched between Barrat and Bosniak.

She pressed the trash can symbol. Delete. Delete. Every business-like message that hid the truth. Delete. Delete. The two-and-a-half-year email trail. Delete. Delete. Delete! Block sender!

Ha!

He was gone. The man who'd waited for her in Rosie's Bar. Who'd cradled her head after they'd made love. Who'd held a tissue to her nose and asked her to blow.

Gone.

Lisa could have this imposter.

Her parents rang to tell her they'd be coming over to watch her graduate. Her father was like an excited school boy.

"Make sure you order your cap and gown in time, Monisha. That shop gets busy!"

Then her mother grabbed the receiver.

"Congratulations, beti… It's lovely and all, but I would be happier if there were three different letters beside your name."

Monisha sighed.

"You know… M, R and S."

44

The weekly 'educational event' happened every Friday night: a sponsored slideshow, followed by a free meal. In the foyer, a crowd of medics swarmed round the pharma rep with the invites. Monisha flung off her white coat, took a flyer and decided to join them. After all, she had nothing better to do. And eight weeks in oncology had taught her that life was short.

There were only twenty minutes to shower and change before the taxi would arrive. Frantically, Monisha scoured her closet looking for what to wear. Purple or cream? Open neck or high neck? Did it really matter? How many women on the cancer ward wished they hadn't spent so much time fussing? She threw on a blouse, flicked her sweaty hair into an updo and catapulted out through the front door.

The meeting was at the Oyster Tavern, five minutes away by cab. As Monisha made her way up the stone steps to the restaurant, a man ran up behind her. He paused momentarily, to look her up and down, twirling his eyes as he did. But then he pushed past her and walked straight in. Weird!

She watched him scuttle to the back of the room. Six foot tall, with brown, wispy hair. Hands in the pockets of his leather jacket. He wore tight, black jeans, while the others wore ties and jackets. He found an empty table at the back and sat down.

The presentation had already begun. A cardiologist flicked through PowerPoint slides emblazoned with drug company logos. He stopped when he noticed Monisha in the doorway.

"Do you wanna take a seat next to Dr Wilton?" he asked, pointing at the man in the leather jacket.

"Cos nobody else does!"

There were peals of laughter. She blushed and made her way to the back. The ogling man extended his clammy hand and handed her a business card.

"Michael Wilton, interventional cardiologist," he whispered.

"Monisha Bastikar, oncology resident."

He turned up his nose. What was an oncologist doing at a lecture on heart disease? She looked him straight in the eye and noticed that he was thin. So thin that his clavicles stood out underneath his t-shirt.

"Hoping to eat lobster."

The man chuckled. One by one, the slides flashed up. Cholesterol. Blood vessels. Monisha's eyes swam with boredom. Until a plate of giant prawns roused her interest.

The lecture finally ended. Michael Wilton called the waiter over and asked him to bring the prawns over.

"Let's see how you do," he said. As if it were a competition.

Monisha began deshelling prawns and slipping them casually into her mouth. Michael Wilton picked at a couple.

He asked her where she'd qualified. She told him about medical school, residency at St Anthony's and the PhD. He nodded and seemed impressed. Waiters flew past them, with plates of onion rings and prawns in batter. Michael Wilton ignored them.

"Let's cut to the chase. What are you doing on Saturday night?"

Monisha stared at him, incredulously.

A fast mover. Unlike John Davidson, with the slow burn.

"I haven't decided yet."

He dipped his middle finger into a plate of balsamic vinegar and licked it.

"Oh! That's what people say when they have nothing to do."

Obnoxious too! She bit her lip. He asked her to call him if she wanted to hook up. Monisha folded her arms. Saturday night? Her parents would be at a dinner party, Swanker at a club and Tina curled up with her husband. What would she be doing? Nothing. Absolutely nothing! But she wouldn't tell him that.

She shrugged her shoulders.

"If I'm not busy, I'll come out… but you have to call me."

He took her number and nodded.

Saturday was grey and drizzly. At seven o'clock, a scarlet convertible pulled up outside her window. Michael

Wilton clambered out, wearing the same leather jacket and a baseball cap, backwards. Monisha ran out through the front door to meet him.

He opened his car door, but there was nowhere to sit. The passenger seat was stacked with CDs, movie magazines and empty Coke cans. He brushed them onto the floor with his hand. Now there was no room for her legs.

A track from the Rolling Stones blasted out of his car window. Michael Wilton drove one handed, eyeing up other women as he went. The car bumped and ground along in the slow zone, before it screeched to a halt in front of a parking lot. Harsh misogynistic lyrics and tinkly xylophone reverberated in her ears.

"Ouch," screamed Monisha as a CD scraped her leg.

Michael Wilton ignored her. He switched the engine off, threw the keys over to the valet, climbed out of his car and began walking. Monisha remained stuck inside, her exit blocked by the stash of CDs. The valet came to her rescue.

"Can't you get up?" sneered Michael Wilton as he headed towards a sports bar.

On either side, the road beckoned. She could cut her losses. Run off this minute and hail a cab. But she was only here to wipe away the memory of John Davidson. Carry on.

Just carry on.

The bar reeked of trainers and testosterone. Michael Wilton sat himself amidst a wall of men, in front of the giant screen. She climbed onto a stool next to him. Her feet dangled awkwardly.

He ordered a couple of beers and kept his eyes glued to the football. At half-time, he opened his mouth to speak.

"Unblocked some tight coronaries this morning and saved some women from becoming widows. So... what have you done?"

Monisha shrugged her shoulders. She told him she'd cleaned her apartment.

Michael Wilton turned up his nose and looked up at the screen again.

"Complete waste of time. I never bother. So... why aren't you married?"

For a brief second Mrs Kulkarni and Shailesh flashed before her. Then Ayesha and Seema. All sandwiched together in that cramped flat.

"I was... once".

When the game finished Michael Wilton spoke about his last girlfriend. A cardiologist from Brisbane, with strict Indian parents. Apparently a virgin, before he used his 'dilator'.

Ugh! Ugh! Ugh! Monisha called the waitress over, ordered another beer and studied her phone. Not a single message. Not one!

Just Michael Wilton's merciless monologue. Drumming through her ears like tinnitus. Each sentence punctuated with a sinister smile.

"I've been out with some beautiful women, you know. Joanne was a dentist, Heidi had a fruit fetish and Anya was a cardiology resident with a degree in gymnastics. That came in handy!"

Monisha screwed up her face.

"Is there really a degree in gymnastics?"

Michael Wilton ignored the question, and launched into a description of parties in Vegas and the lap dancers with clitoral studs.

Monisha closed her eyes, threw a handful of nuts into her mouth and began crunching. Loudly. And, all of a sudden, John Davidson was in front of her, putting his arms round her naked waist and planting feathery kisses on her neck.

Was she using John Davidson to blank out Michael Wilton or vice versa?

There was only one cure for this.

A lurid cocktail. Of hate sex and revenge sex.

Harsh and bitter. Like a vesper Martini.

She lifted her glass.

"Cut the crap. Your place or mine?"

His green eyes glowed with self-satisfaction.

"Really? That quick?"

Monisha looked at the floor and nodded.

They made the twenty-minute journey to his house on foot, because Michael Wilton was too drunk to drive and too tight to pay for a cab. He fumbled with the key.

His apartment was cold and bare. With a splintery wooden floor, a hair-filled double bed in the living room and a shag pile rug buried under a mountain of t-shirts and CDs. All of them labelled 'The Rolling Stones'.

She tossed her clothes into the heap and lay on the bed with her eyes closed, trying to imagine John Davidson's chiselled jaw. His soft, buttery skin. Instead, Michael Wilton's giraffe-like neck twisted round hers and his clavicles dug into her side.

"Oh!" she screamed when he came. "Oh! Oh!"

Oh, she was glad it was over!

Michael Wilton sprang up, yanked his condom off and tied it into a knot before running off to flush it down the toilet.

"Nice jugs," he called as she headed for the shower. "May I join you?"

She shrugged her shoulders.

He rubbed her back with cheap soap, like dish-washing liquid. With his spindly fingers, he tried to touch her breasts. But Monisha jumped out, and found her clothes and a musty smelling towel.

Michael Wilton came out and switched on the hall light. There was Monisha, standing under a row of impressionist prints. Fully clothed.

"What are you doing?"

She was about to call a cab.

His boldness withered.

"Don't you want to stay?"

She shook her head and pressed the speed dial.

"Why? To listen to your godawful stories?"

For a moment, there was silence. He placed a clammy arm on hers.

"We've all been hurt, ya know. Sorry."

She wasn't falling for it. No.

A horn tooted outside. Monisha turned and said goodbye. Michael Wilton managed a rueful smile.

Rain spattered down the windows of the cab. Her stomach rumbled loudly. It was only half past ten. That cheap skate hadn't even bought her dinner! She'd make herself some toast when she got back. Butter it thick.

A man's voice interrupted her thoughts: the cab driver's.

"Are you finished for the night or still working… cos if you're available…"

Oh God! Oh God!

"I'm a cancer doctor! I work at University Hospital!"

In the rear-view mirror, she caught a glimpse of the man's bushy beard and his bulbous nose. He made a garbled apology.

Monisha got out, a block before her apartment.

The ride, he said, was free.

45

It was seven o'clock, handover time on Veritas ward. The staff room was brimming with nurses. And, while the day team were itching to get away, the night team were itching for gossip. News was spreading like wildfire. Somebody had spotted Dr Bastikar out in town with Dr Wilton.

When they got to the last patient, the senior nurse pulled Monisha over and whispered in her ear.

"Wear a condom… two if you can!"

Even on the oncology ward, everyone knew Michael Wilton; the stories began pouring in. He was tight with money and liked to stash his cash. He thought women were gold diggers, and that expensive dinners, marriage and kids were a con. He spent his free time on short-lived flings with almost every woman in the hospital: Nurses. Doctors. Waitresses. Janitors. And even the old lady at the gift shop, who had cheeks that sagged worse than a bulldog's.

"Two X chromosomes is the only requirement," said Nina, the chubby African-American deputy, shaking her head. "You can do better than that."

Monisha shuddered, while the nurses chuckled amongst themselves.

"It was one date! Just one date!" she protested, holding up her index finger.

The double doors flung open. She walked briskly, through the foyer and into the car park, trying to shake the memories out of her head. But, like loose stones, they rattled. And, instead, Michael Wilton's antics began to fascinate her.

Because the girls had also said they'd go to him first for any heart problem. He was, quite honestly, the best. Caring too and not just a money grabber. For many patients, he waived his fee. Momentarily, Michael Wilton went up in her estimation. Until she saw his scarlet convertible parked outside her apartment.

He jumped out, sucking a lollipop, the giant tongue on his Stones t-shirt quivering in the breeze. He pulled out a candy bar from each pocket and handed it to her.

"I bought you some dinner."

She couldn't help but laugh.

He opened his car boot.

"And dessert as well."

A tub of Ben and Jerry's emerged. Chocolate chip.

Monisha stood motionless on the pavement with the keys in her hand. She folded her arms. *What was he trying to do?*

"Could I at least put it in a freezer before it melts, please?"

That same voice! Dejected. Apologetic. Like he'd sounded when she was ready to leave his house. She nodded, half-heartedly.

Within a few minutes, they were both inside. He looked around, and noticed the new Roman blinds and polished hardwood floors.

"Nice place you have here."

Then he screwed up his nose.

"But what's that smell?"

It was the vegetable pilaf and chicken curry she'd cooked in the morning, ready for later. Pungent scents of cumin and cardamom permeated the room as she warmed it up. When it was ready, she dished it onto a plate. Without even asking, Michael Wilton began tucking in. Using his spindly fingers, licking his hands, and spilling grease and turmeric over the work top. With the same spoon, he started on the ice cream.

Monisha watched in shock, arms folded. Furious at how he'd just swooped in.

Like a prairie falcon.

She fumbled for the right words, the right phrase, knowing full well that whatever she chose would be awful and unpalatable.

"Michael… I'm not sure we should take things further."

The slurping noises stopped. He looked up from his carton of chocolate chip. His big green eyes shining. Filled with hurt.

"Why?"

Because you are an absolute Neanderthal.

The thought charged through her brain, but she bit her tongue. She told him that she knew his history with women, and that only heartache lay ahead. His eyebrows arched into a giant frown. Anger flashed across his face. His eyes fired up like sparklers.

Then he spat out the words, punctuating them with droplets of saliva. "A lot of the stuff those gossiping bitches say is not true."

Monisha stared at him quietly. Thoughts clouded up in her mind and eventually became dense fog. There he sat, on her dining chair, drowning in an oversized, un-ironed, tongue t-shirt, rocking back and forth. His wispy brown hair fell onto his forehead. He looked at her, imploringly, his face like a little boy's.

"Perhaps it's because I haven't met the right person."

Now she felt completely guilty. He handed her the carton of ice cream; it was half empty – or half full.

"Could we start again? I'd like to take you somewhere special."

She rolled her eyes. He probably said that to all of them! Hunger pangs griped away in her stomach. She dug out a spoonful of ice cream.

"Just this once."

A few minutes later they were soaring through the Killington Twist at breakneck speed, gazing out at Echo Lake, while the Stones blasted through his sunroof.

And those guys didn't just sing about sex either. There were mournful songs about women growing old and love gone wrong. There were gospel tunes and Latin beats, even a bluesy number about the Boston Strangler.

Michael Wilton turned out to be quite a raconteur. He knew about politics, history and every current event. He'd memorised snippets from PBS shows that aired late at night, about civil rights and the Kennedys. The ones no one else watched. In spite of his awkwardness and odd ways, she was learning new things, every minute. More than she had in five years with Shailesh and John.

Maybe she should see him again. There was nothing to lose.

Or was there?

That night she phoned Tina and told her the story of that dreadful date with Michael Wilton. And how she'd tried to end things. Unsuccessfully.

"Just see where it takes you," was all Tina said.

Normally Tina would have teased out every detail, passed comments and made suggestions. But, now that they were trying for a baby, she had other things on her mind. Like when she was ovulating and making sure Justin was around then.

46

Outside, the dreary winter clouds drifted across the murky sky. Monisha stared into her bedroom mirror. She couldn't quite believe that the woman looking back was thirty-five years old. With a medical degree, a PhD and a divorce under her belt. While her once boozy and promiscuous best friend was married. Gulp!

Monisha looked even harder, her nose almost touching the glass. There weren't any lines on her face or grey hairs. She lifted up her blouse. Yeah, the trips to the gym had kept her body pert enough. But time was slipping away. And, at the rate things were going, she wondered if she would ever marry again.

What the hell had she done with all those years? Taken a blind leap into the unknown with Shailesh. Then another blind leap when she left him. And what had it got her? One night with Joseph Friedman, and two years with a married man, who'd promised her the earth, then moved interstate and changed personality.

And now Michael Wilton. Intriguing, infuriating Michael Wilton. Who was so unstable, that she didn't know where she was from one minute to the next.

If she texted him or rang, he took a day or two to answer. He'd say he'd been in the cardiac lab and run off his feet. Shortly after replying, he'd turn up on her doorstep with clothes for the next day, then stretch himself out on the couch, snatch the remote and turn on PBS.

During his stay, he always managed to empty out her fridge. Lasagne. Curries. Casseroles. Everything she'd made from scratch and cooked ahead. Afterwards he'd work his way through the freshly picked peaches, blueberries and cherry tomatoes she'd bought at the farmer's market. All of it gone in seconds.

At his own place, he lived on junk food and cola. When he wolfed down crisps and candy, she'd scold him. It seemed a strange diet for a cardiologist.

He'd shrug his shoulders.

"Not if you want to die at fifty."

If she asked why, he'd say it was because that was when your 'parts' stopped working. Then he'd ask her to strip off, so he could check that his parts were still working.

She would make him shower before they made love. She bought him expensive gels and soaps to eliminate the stench of potato crisps and gym sweat, but he only showered when he wanted to. And, after they made love, he always yanked off the condom and flushed it down the toilet, immediately. Because women were gold diggers. And kids were just a ploy to get at his money.

She knew little about his family. He was an only child, descended from what he referred to as 'poor white trash'. His mother was somewhere in California, following around faith healers. His father was an alcoholic, and long dead.

When he spoke of his parents, his eyes blazed with hatred. When it all became too much, he'd reach for the CD player and turn on the Stones.

She'd been to concerts with him. In Pittsburgh, Toronto, Montreal and Arizona. She'd even met the 'family'.

The 'family' were a bunch of diehard Stones fans: aging, male hippies, with good jobs, fat wallets and no children. One of his 'brothers' had seen them 150 times and knew the lyrics better than Jagger. Another guy draped every inch of his body in Stones merchandise. Caps, underwear, t-shirts, tongue-pins, jackets, the lot. And one had even worn ear-plugs to see Elton John to preserve his hearing for when the Stones played the next day.

Before and after concerts, the 'family' hung out together. They shared their stories, ate pizza and exchanged warm, drunken hugs. Monisha found herself tagging along for the ride and eventually she began to have fun.

But the 'family' only came together when the Stones played. If there was no tour they didn't see each other for months. Years even. All of them simply evaporated into cyberspace and their relationship was whittled down to a few glum posts on a website.

Her relationship with Michael Wilton followed the same arc. A flurry of texts and visits before a show. Excitement. Pyrotechnics. Then days or weeks of nothing.

Thankfully her work was all consuming. She was starting a new placement in 'solid tumours' with different bosses. In the evenings she led the revision group for board exams. But above all this came the demands of the frontline, that bloody battlefield she visited every day: the oncology ward.

However distasteful things were in her private life, Michael Wilton provided a distraction. A temporary escape from the dark world of cancer and the trail of devastation it left behind. And, just like John Davidson had said, without lab work and research, clinical oncology was soul destroying.

On some days she left for home, weeping helplessly. Usually because they'd lost a young mother, a teenager or, even worse, someone who'd just been given the 'all clear'.

If Michael Wilton showed up, to watch PBS, play a few songs and discuss Chappaquiddick, she'd feel better. And, after some time, the fridge raiding and vinegary gym socks were forgiven and forgotten about.

47

Tina was pregnant. Her once neat strawberry-blonde hair was now red, curly and chemical-free. Her forehead was splotchy from chloasma marks. She paired stretchy slacks with crop tops, belched between sentences and was back on the gluten. But, most astoundingly, her taut, gym-bunny derriere had tripled in size. And she couldn't give a monkey's. Neither did Justin. Because Tina was carrying *his* child.

Monisha yearned for babies too. Lately, when she strolled through the park, her eyes flicked past the fiery birches, and onto the swings and sand pit. A wistful feeling came over her when saw a mother pushing a pram. And, of course, every time she met Tina. Right now, her only hope was to have Michael Wilton's baby, no matter what he'd said.

In her head, she devised a plan. She'd make a pin-prick in a condom and create the teeniest hole. But then she remembered that he used his own condoms, and he kept them on him at all times.

Plan B was equally duplicitous. She'd get him drunk. They'd have bumping, grinding, condom-splitting sex. Except that it was never that bumpy. Or grindy.

One Saturday afternoon, Michael Wilton had barely made it through the front door when she whipped off her clothes and launched herself onto him with a flying leap.

"Whoa," he cried, reaching for a condom from his pocket. She kept him going, for almost an hour, until she was red raw and he looked as though he might collapse.

But when it was over he sat up with a jolt. She watched with horror as he performed the same gruesome routine. Yanking off the slippery rubber. Inspecting the ejaculate. Twirling the condom into a knot and taking it to the bathroom himself.

The sound of the flush made her scream. He didn't notice.

Moments later Michael lay sprawled out on the L-shaped couch, clutching a beer. He seemed mesmerised by the latest offering from PBS: a programme on hidden treasures in the White House.

Monisha threw on her towelling robe and tiptoed in. Eventually she asked herself a painful question. Was this how it was going to be, year upon year? Him lounging about in his underwear slurping beer and she, his faithful food shopper and fridge stocker. Hanging out in hope for the next rock concert.

Like hot stew in a crockpot, the resentment bubbled away inside her. After a few minutes, Monisha marched over to the TV screen and stood in front of it. With her hands on her hips, she blocked his view of the White House.

"Don't you *ever* want to settle down, Michael?"

He arched himself round so he could see. She stretched her arms out wide and made it impossible.

"You're just… *never* going to have kids?"

Michael Wilton shot up and threw the empty beer can onto the floor. Two droplets of amber liquid fell onto her pristine rug. Then he glared at her, his eyes turning a murky green.

"Here we fucking go! It's that friend of yours, isn't it? The one who looks like a beached whale now."

"At least she's happy!" said Monisha. "And so is her husband."

He began laughing, an evil, mocking laugh. Then he spat out his words like viper venom.

"Well, he won't be when it's out. Fucking her will be like fucking the Grand Canyon!"

Monisha froze in front of the screen, her eyes welling up. Michael Wilton continued his foul-mouthed rant, with his arms waving and his fingers pointing.

"And they won't be able to go anywhere when the kid is born. She'll be one of those fucking psychos with a nanny-cam! They could never go to see the Stones, like we do."

Monisha let out an exasperated groan.

"The Stones have kids Michael. They're still having kids!"

"That's because they earn shitloads of money."

"You've FUNDED them, Michael. You've funded their kids. You and Ray and Chuck. The whole crazy, fucked-up lot of you!"

Michael Wilton looked up blankly, dumbstruck by the suggestion. Flummoxed, in spite of his Ivy League degree.

Monisha marched over to the couch and snatched the remote control from his hands. She pointed it at the TV. After a brief silence, her voice echoed from within the fur-lined prison cell. But this time it sounded different: calm, clear and determined. It was the same voice which had told Mrs Kulkarni that she wouldn't be staying for breakfast, that she was leaving the marriage.

"Well, I'll be having a child, Michael. With you or without you. And sooner, rather than later."

Michael Wilton shuddered. His green eyes slowly began fogging up. It was a familiar sound, that death rattle that spelled the end. After all the flapping and whirling, another one would get away. She'd disappear into a murky underworld filled with ludicrous things, like baby showers. And he'd be off to the sports bar again with yet another willing victim.

He rushed to the door, trouser legs only half way up. "GO FUCK UP YOUR LIFE THEN!"

"FINE, I WILL!" screamed Monisha through the open doorway.

She slammed the door and immediately turned to look at the clock on the oven. Her heart was fluttering. She clutched her chest and took in a breath.

Think, think, what time was it now in Mumbai?

The Dases would be at Sitara Road this weekend and afterwards they'd be heading back to Vermont with her parents. A big job lay ahead for the Bastikar family now. The Adam Court house was going up for sale.

Monisha pressed the numbers on a touchphone. She could not do this on Skype, there were too many onlookers. A helper answered.

"Could I speak to Aunty Swati please?"

Amidst the crackling noises she heard a weary "Hello."

"Aunty Swati, what do you think about me having a baby with a sperm donor? You could be its grandmother… Well, one of the grandmothers!"

The shocked silence came like a kick in the guts. Hours seemed to pass.

"I think that's a wonderful idea, Monisha! We'll, er… um… bake that cake together when I get back. Right now, your mom wants a word."

Oh God! Oh God! Poor Aunty Swati. It must have been all the people hovering round.

"Monisha, are you well?" screeched Leela Bastikar.

"Yep fine."

Her mother would die when she heard! She could conceal it. Say nothing until she was showing. A grown woman didn't need permission from her mother to get pregnant. Unless it didn't work and she had to adopt. Her mother might have to provide a character reference. She'd have to be super nice to her from now on.

"Did you remember to ring the carpenter?" asked Mrs Bastikar.

Damn! She'd forgotten.

"Why not? We reminded you!"

Why not? Because the wards were full of cancer. Because Tina was having a baby. And, because when she'd wanted one, Michael Wilton had just upped and left.

48

Twenty-three Adam Court was going up for sale. Its only tenants, a newly arrived Indian family, had long gone. Swanker was using it as a crash pad until his transfer to Chicago. And he hadn't exactly kept it tidy; because, he said, it was more like a time capsule than a house. It badly needed renovating. The yard was littered with fallen trees from last year's storms. The garage was stuffed with boxes of their childhood things. The avocado bathroom suite had to go. And the ground floor was crying out for a kitchen-diner.

When the Bastikars had pitched the place as an 'attractive project', the realtors weren't interested. If the work wasn't done, the house wouldn't sell.

Aunt Romila helped stir things up by suggesting to her sister that a few months in the States to supervise the renovation would 'do everyone a world of good'. Uncle Shyam and Uncle Rohit rarely visited Sitara Road now;

they were getting tired of their non-resident relatives incessantly moaning about Mumbai.

Consequently, Leela and Amit Bastikar found themselves in the uncomfortable position of having to travel back to Vermont, in the lead up to winter, to spend time and money on a house that they would never live in, destroying countless precious memories in the process. But it had to be done. Without the money, how could they ever downsize into a flat? Or more importantly, afford Swanker's wedding.

One Sunday morning, a few days after they arrived, Mrs Bastikar asked the Dases over to help strip wallpaper. Outside, thick rain clouds were gathering; the drizzle was due anytime soon. The Dases came early, but after breakfast and coffee, progress was slow.

Swanker was busy making trips to the dump. Professor Bastikar had to be driven to the drug store when he hurt his shoulder. Ultimately, Mrs Bastikar, Monisha and Aunty Swati were left holding the sponges. They started in the master bedroom, two scraping, one steaming.

The room was dusty and dated, the queen-sized bed adorned with a chintz cover and crocheted cushions. There was a single picture on the wall that the tenants hadn't taken down: a family photograph of Amit Bastikar in a suit, carrying four-year-old Swanker on one hip. Mrs Bastikar stood next to him in burnt orange silk, with her arm wrapped around Monisha, who wore a pink, puffy dress and a bow in her hair.

Aunty Swati stood on the foot stool and ran the scraper along the wall opposite the photograph. Half an hour in, she'd worked up a sweat.

"How's Michael Wilton?" she suddenly asked. "It must have been a year now at least."

Monisha tried to block out the image of him running out through the front door while still putting on his jeans. She rolled the steamer up and down with heavier strokes.

"He didn't want marriage… or kids."

Leela Bastikar dropped her wet sponge and picked up a scraper, all the while she stared incredulously at Monisha.

"Why waste time with someone like that when there are thousands of guys who do?"

Monisha sighed and shook her head. A square of vintage, floral wallpaper curled and flopped into her hands. Neatly and simply, unlike anything else in her life.

"There are thousands of guys who don't want kids, Mom, and thousands who want them, have them and leave them. The rest are a minority."

Aunty Swati interrupted. "What's the point of getting married, just to be controlled by someone else? If I were her age, I'd be dating lots of men." She paused, then raised her voice above the harsh scraping noises. "These days you can even have a child on your own."

Monisha felt a rush of butterflies swirling round her stomach. This was it. Aunty Swati was doing as promised; she was baking the cake.

Leela Bastikar shrieked. "Hai Ram! What are you talking about, Swati? What sort of ideas are you planting in her head?"

Suddenly Swati Das was livid. Her eyes swelled with rage, until they were almost ready to pop out of their sockets. Thirty years of childlessness had prepared her for this moment. A lifetime spent attending christenings, birthdays, sacred thread ceremonies and graduations. With nothing to show of her own.

She flung the scraper onto the floor and met her friend's gaze.

"YOU WOULDN'T HAVE A CLUE WHAT I'M TALKING ABOUT LEELA, BECAUSE YOU HAVEN'T FACED WHAT I'VE FACED!"

A bone-chilling silence swept the room. Seconds turned swiftly into minutes. Swati Das sat herself down on the foot stool. Her oversized, paint-stained shirt hung limply round her toned legs. Her unlined face and the odd strand of grey in her jet-black hair glimmered under the ceiling lights. At fifty-four, she found herself wandering adrift, in a middle-aged wasteland. A strange time in a woman's life.

Like three o'clock, too late for lunch, but far too early for tea or dinner.

Stone-faced, she recounted the lurid details of her picture-perfect marriage. It was Saurav's fault they were childless, all because of his 'failing testicles'. They'd visited fertility clinics, but he'd backed out of using donor sperm. And, when she desperately wanted to adopt, he wasn't interested. He would never have left his practice to go scouting round orphanages in India. And he knew darn well the authorities wouldn't let her do it alone.

Throughout the years, Swati Das had suffered in silence. He had his 'medicine', she had her dead-end bank job. On weekends she doled out the invites. Played charming hostess and dutiful wife. Everybody loved the Dases, especially Saurav, so handsome and witty! The couple's closeness was enviable; they finished each other's sentences.

Twice she'd taken an overdose. Saurav pumped her stomach himself, so it never got out.

She was resigned to her fate; her mother had said. Paying a hefty price for her attractive, adoring husband, and inextricably bound to him for seven lives.

Leela Bastikar wiped her eyes. Then she shuffled over to her friend, and extended one arm, ready to place it round her shoulders. But Swati Das shook her head vehemently and resisted.

"If I were Monisha's age, Leela, I would have left long ago. And if I couldn't find a man, I'd get a sperm donor."

Leela Bastikar raised her eyebrows. Eventually, she managed a hesitant nod. Monisha put aside the stepladder and placed herself between the two women. Her stomach began churning. She took in a breath, sharp and quick.

"Mom... I want a baby. I'm almost thirty-six now. My eggs are running out. If I wait for the right man, it may never happen."

She paused, in anticipation of her mother's reply. When none came Monisha took in another breath, deeper this time.

"So, I'm going to try with a sperm donor, and if it doesn't work, I'll adopt. Either way I'll be a mom and Aunty Swati can be a grandmother too."

Leela Bastikar froze, then clutched her chest. She could not bring herself to look at her daughter, nor her best friend. Instead, she stared down at the floor, where the vintage, floral wallpaper, with its purple pansies and blood-red roses, lay in tatters round her feet. Out of the blue, a flood of memories came bursting through.

Thirty-five years ago, she'd held her new baby daughter. Curled one finger round her tiny toes. She hadn't known whether she was having a boy or a girl. They'd bought this wallpaper on their way home from the hospital. Then Amit read somewhere that nurseries should be soothing places and not too bright. So, they'd kept it for their own room.

Three years later, her beloved baby boy arrived and with him the congratulatory telegram from her overjoyed parents; Swanker was their first grandson.

Leela Bastikar lifted her head. Her eye caught the photograph on the wall, taken when the kids were four and seven. Oh, those sacred days! Of balloons and bubble baths. Cut knees and falling teeth. Endless trips between swimming pools and skating rinks.

And to think that whenever Saurav Das announced he was taking his wife on a luxury cruise, she'd actually felt jealous! When all along it was Swati who'd missed out on the most incredible journey.

Mrs Bastikar placed her arms round Monisha and Swati. Weeping and blubbering, she clasped them both tightly.

"I've been blessed. So blessed! Who am I to stop you, Monisha? And how could I stop our beloved Swati from becoming a grandmother?"

Monisha raised her eyes to the heavens and murmured a 'thank you'. For a few moments the women sat with their arms linked together. Leela Bastikar and Swati reminisced about their first time in the States. How their itchy wool coats slung over their chiffon saris did little to block out the teeth-chattering cold. And how miserable they'd felt, relegated to an ice box like Vermont, when many of their friends had made it to LA.

The sounds of the car pulling up and the tread of male feet on the staircase eventually prised them apart. Amit Bastikar pulled the bedroom door open and saw the ladies sitting cross-legged on the floor.

"What's going on here?" he asked.

Swati Das grinned like a Cheshire cat.

"Nothing!" said Monisha.

Leela Bastikar looked at her husband and shrugged her shoulders. Then a thought crept into her head, one she'd keep silent for now. If Monisha was going to have a baby, they would have to return to Vermont. That meant they could keep this house and raise their grandchild, where their own children had grown up, at twenty-three Adam Court.

"Nothing," she added, after some time.

"I can see that," said Amit Bastikar eyeing up the half-finished job.

Leela Bastikar opened her mouth to say something, then held back in frustration. She couldn't tell her husband to stick to E equals MC^2. He had retired now.

That afternoon, when Monisha reached her own apartment, there was one all-consuming thought attacking her brain like a virus. She was going to try for a baby.

A baby! A baby! A baby!

She opened up her cupboard and reached in the corner hoping to find a pair of jogging bottoms. Instead, she pulled out three Rolling Stones t-shirts, a pair of black jeans and a crumpled-up work shirt.

Michael Wilton's stuff was still in her house, reeking of vinegary sweat and negative energy. Ugh! It had to go, all of it. Right this minute.

Monisha tossed his things into a carrier bag and made her way to the hospital.

The ride took five minutes on a Sunday.

The cardiac unit was packed with nurses and visitors. Patients on trolleys whizzed by. She inched her way through the crowd and headed for a side room. The nurses recognised her and let her pass. The door to Michael Wilton's office was ajar. She knocked.

"Come in."

His voice seemed friendly enough, but when he saw her, his eyebrows knotted together and his face reddened. He noticed the garbage bag and the black jeans sticking out from the top. Then he let out a gruff noise, a semi-roar, the kind of noise that an ogre would make in a fairy tale. An aggrieved, misunderstood ogre.

Once upon a time, the noise would have unnerved her. She didn't want to hurt his feelings. She would have apologised, and fumbled through an explanation about the family home being renovated and how she needed to clear out her wardrobe. Once upon a time she would have even said 'yes' to a coffee and a chat. But now she had to protect her body and her mind.

Now she had to create a safe space for her baby.

"Your stuff," she said quietly, before slipping out.

On her way back, Monisha glanced towards the nurses' station. The girls seemed busy. One peered at a medicine chart, another one walked round with a phone hooked to her ear. She decided not to stop and walked past.

Seconds later, several slow, thunderously loud clapping noises stopped her in her tracks and made her turn round. It was chubby Nina. She'd been watching all along.

49

The walls of Finchley Fertility Clinic were plastered with baby photos. Of newborns and toddlers, twins and triplets. Wrapped in blankets, dressed as bunnies, coming out of boxes and eggs. In pink, blue and green pastel colours, handknitted or with sewn on patchwork lettering. Monisha squinted to look at them one by one. There were no Indian babies.

If this worked, hers would be the first.

Today was implantation day. The day on which the magic could or might not happen.

Tina had offered to come with her, but right now she wanted to be alone. So far, Tina had been great. They'd filled in the first questionnaire together, giggling at the irony. They'd trawled through the lists of men, in search of Mr Right Sperm, like her mother had trawled through the matrimonial columns once upon a time.

They'd spent ages studying heights, occupations, hair colour and eye colour. Like kids at a candy store, they'd been captivated by the choices: sporty, musical, academic or all three. A computer buff who played the drums and ran marathons. A scientist who sang R 'n' B. Black hair, chestnut brown or blond. It was all too much!

Ultimately, they'd decided that the child should look like the mother. And, because there were no Indian donors, they'd chosen a Hispanic donor. Moreover, as Monisha always wanted a doctor for a husband, they went for a medical student. His ice-hockey playing and taut abs were a bonus.

The female doctors had waiting lists a mile long and they didn't pull favours. So, she'd booked in with the man: thirty something, scruffy and laid back.

But nothing had prepared her for the rollercoaster ride.

At her first appointment, he'd taken her details and shrugged his shoulders. Her periods were regular, she could take a couple of shots at insemination. At a few hundred dollars a pop it would be cheaper; there'd be no drugs involved. And she might just get lucky.

Get 'lucky' – her?

She'd almost choked to death at the suggestion. So far, she'd never got lucky. Never won anything: not the turkey in a Thanksgiving raffle, not even a furry toy at the arcade.

And cheaper? Not when you factored in the cost of calming the craziness in her head. That constant tirade of 'will it, won't it?', which required acupuncture sessions, zen yoga and chill-out CDs.

They'd settled on two attempts at insemination. Both times, it bombed. There was no choice left but IVF. Expensive, uncomfortable IVF, with this scruff-hound of a doctor.

She'd burst into tears and called Tina. She wanted someone else. She'd wait six months. The clinic in Boston was better.

Tina had been her voice of reason. "No. No and no," she'd said.

The guy had a solid reputation. They should keep the travelling to a minimum. It was the process, not the clinic. The drugs were the same. These places were sprouting up everywhere now. You could have fertility treatment anywhere in the world!

So, she'd stuck with the scruff-hound and taken on extra shifts at the hospital to pay him. Swanker had put in $1,000 of 'unpaid rent'. And he'd even driven out in heavy snow to pick up a batch of injections. After all it was in his favour. With a grandchild to fuss over, his folks would stop 'bugging him to get married'.

Her mother had tolerated her hormone driven-mood swings, even though it was like having 'teenage Monisha' back. And it was Aunty Swati who'd taken the call from the lab technician with the results. When she'd been hanging off the edge of her seat, too nervy to speak.

Ten follicles. Eight eggs. But only four good embryos. *Four out of eight. Aargh!*

She'd hit the floor. Until once more Tina came to the rescue.

"It only takes one good embryo, Monisha... just one!"

And to remind her, she had the words printed on a t-shirt: 'JUST ONE'.

In fact, out of all of them, it was only her father who'd balked, after he'd searched the internet, and found out about failure rates and cancer risk.

"But the biggest problem is that the child won't have a father. And what happens when they're eighteen and they want to find out?" he'd asked.

She wasn't bothered. Eighteen was light years away.

"What are you going to do on Father's Day every year?"

That one freaked her. What was she going to do on Father's Day?

Draw a sperm on the card?

Suddenly, she was wracked with guilt. She began to realise that it was not going to be plain sailing. That choices had consequences. And that bringing a fatherless child into the world was actually a huge, huge deal.

But, right now, any consequence seemed better than a lifetime of childlessness. The slow dragging misery of having to attend birthdays, graduations and weddings of other people's kids. And to enter the time tunnel of grief, like Aunty Swati.

So, she'd stood up to her father and looked him straight in the eye.

"This was not how I wanted it, Daddy… It's not ideal. But I'm thirty-six now. My eggs won't last, and I can't wait for a man forever."

Then she'd sobbed until it hurt.

"And I can't go on living if I don't at least try."

When he saw his little girl in a flood of tears, Amit Bastikar quit his internet searches, shut down the computer and gave her his blessing.

"Whatever makes you happy, beti," he'd said.

For thirty agonising minutes, she sat on the couch in the waiting room of Finchley Fertility Clinic, leafing through lifestyle magazines and reminiscing about the bittersweet journey through to implantation day. On her quest for happiness.

Finally, the nurse called her name.

"Ms Bastikar, are you ready?"

Monisha smiled and nodded.

She was.

Moments later, she was in the treatment room, half-naked under a paper draw sheet. When the scruff-hound went off to gown up, she folded her hands in prayer and closed her eyes.

A myriad of images flashed forth. Silently she mouthed the words.

"Divine mother goddesses. Durga. Laxmi. Venus. Hail Mary, full of grace. Wherever you are. Whichever world. I beg you all to hear my prayer."

50

A sprinkling of trout lilies and the sweet scent of maple filled the woods. After a long, arduous winter, spring was finally here. Even though nights were still freezing, and the gravel roads were layering up with mud. And even if those pretty, purple lilacs would show themselves for one week only. She was here. Glorious, triumphant spring.

And this spectacular feat of nature happily coincided with the twelve-week mark on Monisha's calendar. Now she'd made it to twelve weeks, she could start telling people about the twins. Her beautiful baby twins!

Not everyone was as ecstatic as she was. She'd fought tooth and nail with Susan Baxter to get the clinical stuff out of the way so she could sail through the rest of the pregnancy perched on a chair with her head behind a microscope, in 'basic haematology'.

And she'd dangled a carrot too. She offered to stay on longer and clear the backlog of unfinished projects that

John Davidson had left behind. Initially he'd promised to collaborate, but between the work in Denver and looking after his children, he just couldn't juggle it all. Especially now that there were three of them.

Susan Baxter had jumped at the chance. A board-certified physician, on a research salary, who could cover a few on-calls if needed? She'd hit the jackpot! For Monisha, abandoning the clinical work meant less stress and more time at home, but money would be tight. Thankfully, the Dases would help with childcare, school fees and medical.

For years, she'd waited in silent hope that, one day, Shailesh would pay back the $30,000 loan or dowry or whatever it was. The money never materialised. Her mother had heard on the grapevine that Shailesh had remarried. The lucky lady was a doctor and ten years younger than herself.

Surprise. Surprise.

When Monisha splashed the ultrasound picture of twin one and twin two onto Facebook, Riya immediately posted a comment.

"Love the babies already! Mom doesn't understand, but makes perfect sense to me. Lol. Congrats ur the 1st doctor in our family and 1st single-baby momma. Lol."

The twenty-week scan was on the day of Lilly May's first birthday party. Monisha decided to call in on the way home. She surveyed Tina and Justin's four-bedroom house from the outside; it was exactly what they hadn't wanted: comfortable and convenient. They preferred a few acres in the countryside, with a swimming pool and mountain view, but, to Monisha, that all seemed plain dumb. Why spend two hours stuck on the I89 each day, away from their baby? Wasn't it better to stay in Burlington in the week and buy a weekend retreat?

As if to prove a point, Lilly May ended up in hospital with bronchitis, and Tina and Justin jumped on this house, a few streets down from the newly refurbished Adam Court, where the Bastikars now lived. And they actually congratulated Monisha for suggesting something so sensible, for a change.

Monisha couldn't help but giggle as she made her way in through their front door. Tina was in her element, flying round the kitchen in a pink apron, her strawberry-blonde curls whitened by the flour from last-minute baking.

"So, come on girl, tell us what you're having!"

Monisha folded her arms and looked away.

"The sonographer wasn't certain."

Justin walked towards her, balancing Lilly May in one arm and a tray of cakes in the other.

"Oh, come on… They must have said!"

Monisha looked at the crowd of unfamiliar adults perched on Tina's environmentally friendly dining chairs and the babies wiggling uncomfortably on their laps. It seemed strange to think that she would be part of this group one day.

They all waited anxiously for her news, but this time there would be no big announcements. No ending up with egg on her face and a truckload of the wrong stuff.

And her mother agreed. She was always complaining that, in this day and age, everybody knew everything. Too much of it. Too soon. And everyone's secrets were out in the open: What they wore to bed, what they ate for lunch. Their baby bumps. Their stretch marks. Their Caesarean scars. Too much information! Or as they said these days: 'TMI!'.

Wasn't there space left in the world for one joyous piece of unexpected news? A wonderful surprise, or, in this case, two?

Monisha sauntered over to the bay window and lifted the voile curtain. She could just make out her mother hobbling down the path, clutching an enormous polka-dot gift box with both hands. Slung over her shoulder was a bag of knitting. With two babies to knit for, her mother and Aunty Swati had been kept quite busy.

Monisha waved through the window and let out a contented sigh. Then she turned back to face her hosts.

"Sorry guys," she said with a smile. "I guess you'll just have to wait and see."

Acknowledgements:

I would like to thank Debbie Alper from the Writer's Workshop for her invaluable teaching sessions on the art of novel writing. Thank you to Julie Evans for formatting the initial manuscript and to Merrill George for the final proof reading. I am grateful for the helpful guidance from my film-maker friend Jaya Macdonald and for the power, positivity and proof-reading efforts of my dear friend Wendy Hussey. Sincere thanks to my beautiful cousin Amrita Sen for letting me use her photograph and to Heidi Hurst, Hannah Dakin and the rest of the production team at Matador. And a hearty thanks to all you readers!

About the author:

Moushmi Biswas is a physician in the NHS. She lives in Wales with her partner, her son and a naughty little dog. This is her first novel.